exampl

Sophia de Mello Breyner Andresen

— ❧ —

exemplary tales

— ❧ —

TRANSLATED FROM THE
PORTUGUESE BY ALEXIS LEVITIN

INTRODUCTION BY
CLÁUDIA PAZOS-ALONSO

Tagus Press   *UMass Dartmouth*   *Dartmouth, Massachusetts*

Tagus Press is the publishing arm of the Center for Portuguese Studies and Culture at the University of Massachusetts Dartmouth.
Center Director: João M. Paraskeva

ADAMASTOR SERIES 10
Tagus Press at UMass Dartmouth
www.portstudies.umassd.edu
Manufactured in the United States of America
General Editor: Frank F. Sousa / Managing Editor: Mario Pereira
Copyedited by Peter W. Fong / Designed by Mindy Basinger Hill
Typeset in Adobe Jenson Pro

For all inquiries, please contact:
Tagus Press
Center for Portuguese Studies and Culture
UMass Dartmouth
285 Old Westport Road
North Dartmouth MA 02747–2300
Tel. 508–999–8255   Fax 508–999–9272
www.portstudies.umassd.edu

FUNDAÇÃO
LUSO-AMERICANA

Publication of this book was made possible in part
by a grant from the Luso-American Foundation

Library of Congress Cataloging-in-Publication Data

Andresen, Sophia de Mello Breyner.
[Contos exemplares. English]
Exemplary tales: Sophia de Mello Breyner Andresen / translated from the
Portuguese by Alexis Levitin; introduction by Cláudia Pazos-Alonso.
pages   cm.— (Adamastor series; 10)
Includes bibliographical references.
ISBN 978-1-933227-66-5 (pbk.: alk. paper)
1. Andresen, Sophia de Mello Breyner—Translations into English.
2. Short stories, Portuguese—Translations into English. I. Levitin, Alexis, translator.
II. Alonso, Cláudia Pazos, writer of introduction. III. Title.
PQ9261.A6893C5813 2015
869.3'42—dc23   2015008582

5   4   3   2   1

— ❧ —

For Francisco

WHO TAUGHT ME

THE COURAGE

AND THE JOY

OF AN UNEQUAL

STRUGGLE

— ❧ —

Heles dado el nombre de
ejemplares, y si bien lo miras no hay ninguna de
quien no se pueda sacar un ejemplo.

CERVANTES

"Prólogo al Lector," *Novelas ejemplares*

contents

—📖—

translator's preface

— ઽ૭ —

Alexis Levitin

Poetry is my first love. In fact, this is only the second book of prose fiction that I have translated from the Portuguese. The first was *Soulstorm* by Brazil's great stylist Clarice Lispector. It consisted of two of her late books: *A Via Crucis do Corpo* and *Onde Estivestes de Noite*. For me, that I have been seduced into the realm of prose only by Clarice and Sophia is not a coincidence. What unites them is clear: both are fundamentally poets, even when they write narratives that appear to be prose. And that poetic quality is what draws me to them. I am in this business for the beauty of language. It is the provocation, the challenge, the reward.

Sophia, of course, is considered one of the major Portuguese poets of the twentieth century. And it is clear that when she turns to prose she does not leave her poetic mantle behind. Her love of nature, of sharply delineated imagery, of *nitidez*, is evident in every sentence. Here are a few examples of the poetic rewards offered the translator of *Exemplary Tales*.

In a narrative based on childhood memories of a beggar wandering along the seacoast, she depicts the mysterious vagabond in these terms: "His curly white beard was like a foaming wave. The thick blue veins of his legs were like the cables of ships. His body was like a mast, and as he walked he swayed like a sailor or a boat. His eyes, like the sea itself, were sometimes blue, sometimes gray, sometimes green, and sometimes I even saw them turn violet." And when he takes his stand atop a dune, "the whole afternoon looked like an enormous transparent flower, spread wide to the horizon." And when he spoke, it was with "words that glistened like the scales of fish, words vast and clean-swept like a beach." This is prose impregnated with the metaphoric freedom of poetry. Her beggar has become a creature of the sea, perhaps a modern remnant of a Greek sea god. And the brief saga resonates with the feelings of both fairy tale and myth.

In her recreation of the story of the three kings, she gives each such a finely wrought humanity and individuality, that the necessity of the long journey towards the Christ child becomes spiritually compelling. Here, for example, is the conclusion to "Melchior":

> And above the world of sleep, above the tangled shadow of dreams in which men were lost groping, as if in a thick, humid, shifting labyrinth, the star, young, tremulous, and bedazzled, was igniting its joy.
> And Melchior left his palace that very night.

After such prose, he had no choice.

I would like to conclude these brief remarks by turning to "The Journey," one of the greatest short stories I have ever read. It is both delicate and hair-raising, touching and shattering. It retells, with crystal transparency, the journey of a life, and one feels caught in a fairy tale and Dante's *Divine Comedy* at the same time. A writer cannot bring us closer to the bliss of ordinary life and the heavy price we all must pay in the end. For me, translating *Exemplary Tales* was a privilege and a joy, but translating "The Journey" was one of the most moving experiences of my forty years as a translator from the Portuguese. Thank you Sophia.

acknowledgments

— ক —

When I first came to Portugal in 1978 to begin translating Portuguese poetry, it was Sophia who welcomed me into her home and into the literary world of her country. For that I remain eternally grateful.

As for the translation of *Exemplary Tales*, I would like to thank Clara Pires of Montreal, whose human wisdom and linguistic acuity guided me during my earliest efforts. I would also like to thank Fernando Beleza, who kindly read the entire manuscript and provided many helpful comments and corrections. In addition, I would like to acknowledge the friendship and support of Sophia's daughter and literary executor, Maria Andresen, who was especially attentive to my problems dealing with Sophia's richly poetic allegory "The Journey." Last, but not least, I must thank once again SUNY-Plattsburgh for its ongoing support of my translation activities.

Acknowledgment is made to the editors of the following literary magazines for prior publication of these stories: *Barnabe Mountain Review, Image, Left Curve, Rosebud,* and *Springhouse Journal.*

—*Alexis Levitin*—

introduction

— ৶ —

A LANDMARK COLLECTION IN
SALAZAR'S PORTUGAL —
SOPHIA'S *EXEMPLARY TALES*

— ৶ —

Cláudia Pazos-Alonso

Sophia de Mello Breyner Andresen (1919–2004) is a legend-
ary figure both in her birth country and throughout the Portuguese-speaking world. More commonly known simply by her
Christian name, which some critics have considered to be predes-
tined (it means wisdom in Greek), Sophia became a cult writer
in her own lifetime and won numerous literary prizes. Her long
and distinguished literary career spanned six decades, thirty years
either side of the 1974 revolution. The spell of her poetry extended
into the English-speaking world in the 1970s,[1] paving the way in
subsequent decades for three anthologies in English devoted to her
work. Despite its iconic status in Portugal, however, *Contos Exemplares*, or *Exemplary Tales*, has not been available to an Anglophone
audience until now.

CONTEXT

Born of aristocratic stock, Sophia spent a happy childhood in Porto, living in Quinta do Campo Alegre, a mansion located on the grounds of what is today the Porto Botanical Garden. In 1936, she enrolled at the University of Lisbon to study classics but—as was the case twenty years earlier, with the short-lived poet Florbela Espanca—she never completed her academic studies. It is tempting to imagine the call of poetry was stronger.

Sophia was one of the few women writers who managed to achieve widespread critical acclaim in pre-1974 Portugal. In 2014, ten years after her death, she became the second woman to be transferred to the Panteão Nacional, alongside the *fado* singer Amália Rodrigues (whose consecration coincided with the dawn of a new century in 2001). With this honor, Sophia effectively acts as a cultural boundary-marker in the construction of the nation, where a few exceptional women, admitted to the canon at the rate of one or two per generation, guarantee "the unity of collective national consciousness and hegemonic cultural memory" (Owen and Pazos Alonso 2011: 21). Her oeuvre and life were particularly suited to fulfill this role, as we shall see.

The first significant public recognition of Sophia's work occurred several decades earlier, when her sixth collection of poetry, *Livro Sexto*, won the Portuguese Writers Society's 1964 prize for poetry. This watershed event nearly coincided with the publication of *Contos Exemplares*, her first short-story collection for adults. Together, these two complementary works brought her to the attention of a wider public, as much for their enduring literary merit as for their ability to verbalize opposition to the values embodied by the Salazar dictatorship. Her estrangement from the regime had been

apparent in her poetry from *No Tempo Dividido* (1954), gathering
momentum in *Mar Novo* (1958), then becoming firmly embedded
in *Livro Sexto* (1962), whose last section contained thinly veiled
attacks on Salazar, portrayed as "The Old Vulture."
Although Sophia's progressive brand of Catholicism increasingly
led her to embrace an outspoken criticism of the status quo, she
was a dissident from within. Her otherwise impeccable credentials
(she was a married mother of five) consequently made it difficult for
the regime to deal with her. After she and her husband Francisco
Sousa Tavares supported Humberto Delgado's 1958 presidential
campaign,[2] however, he lost his job and she was interrogated by
PIDE—the regime's secret police (Castro 2014). Perhaps not entirely coincidentally, Sophia again experienced PIDE surveillance
in the year in which *Livro Sexto* and *Contos Exemplares* were published. In a letter to her friend and fellow poet Jorge de Sena, who
had been living in exile in Brazil since 1959, she wrote: "Como a
PIDE levou de minha casa todas as suas cartas tenho medo que
o correio esteja muito vigiado agora" [Since PIDE has confiscated
all your letters from my house, I fear my mail is now under close
surveillance] (*Correspondência 1959–1978*, 66).
The success of *Livro Sexto*, no doubt fueled partly by the 1964
prize for poetry, resulted in the printing of a second edition that
year. The speech made by Sophia on that occasion (reproduced in
the third edition of 1966) provided her with a golden opportunity
to argue that poetry could not be divorced from (political) reality: "Quem procura uma relação justa com a pedra, com a árvore,
com o rio, é necessariamente levado, pelo espírito de verdade que
o anima, a procurar uma relação justa com o homem. . . . E é por
isso que o poeta é levado a buscar a justiça pela própria natureza
da sua poesia" (7). [Whoever seeks a just relation with a stone, a

tree, a river, is necessarily led by the spirit of truth within to seek a just relation with mankind. . . . And thus the poet is led to seek justice by the very nature of his poetry.]

A similarly passionate revolt in the face of suffering and social injustice runs through *Contos Exemplares*. Like *Livro Sexto*, the collection captured the national mood of the moment: an increasing disquiet. At the time, the single most pressing political issue in Portuguese life was the colonial war, beginning in Angola in 1961, then spreading to Mozambique in 1964. This divisive and bloody conflict lasted more than a decade, until the Salazar/Caetano regime was finally toppled on April 25, 1974. While no direct mention of this war occurs in the tales, their indictment of Salazar's regime soon gained them a place in the country's collective imagination. The book's social importance was broadly equivalent, in the Portuguese context, to the role played in their respective countries by two other iconic collections, both also published in 1964: *We Killed Mangy-Dog* by the Mozambican author Honwana, and *Luuanda* by the Angolan writer Luandino Vieira. Luandino was awarded the 1965 prize for fiction by the Portuguese Writers Society, an honor he famously never received, as PIDE forcibly closed the society after it announced the prize.

A few months later, in October 1965, Sophia was one of the signatories of the "Manifesto dos 101 Católicos," denouncing the collusion between the Catholic Church and the regime in the on-going colonial war.[3] At Christmas that same year, "Os Três Reis do Oriente" (The Three Kings) was published as a freestanding tale by Estudios Cor, with a foreword by the house's literary editor, José Saramago, then a little-known writer. The edition was intended as a Christmas present for friends of the publisher and "Season's Greetings" were offered on the first page. Highlighting Sophia's growing profile as a public intellectual, the tale invoked a Christian

ethos to further the cause of social justice. Saramago's foreword
began by citing the opening line of "A Estrela" (The Star) from *Livro
Sexto*, "Eu caminhei na noite" [I walked in the night]. After suggest-
ing that the role of the poet was to illuminate the darkest night,
Saramago closed with a profession of faith in a future where hope
and love might prevail. The circulation of this tale, articulating the
discontent of the more liberal wing of Christian society, constituted
both an act of resistance and an exercise in consciousness-raising.

Contos Exemplares was republished in 1966 with its original six
stories. The inclusion of "The Three Kings" began with the third
edition (1970), which featured a preface by a well-respected public
figure: the former bishop of Porto, Dom António Ferreira Gomes.
This further contributed to the reception of *Contos Exemplares* as a
resistance text, since Dom António had been forced into a ten-year
exile due to his opposition and allowed to return only after Salazar
was succeeded by Caetano, in 1969.[4]

The 1960s and early 1970s were a politically volatile time in Portugal. Both Sophia and her husband continued to be on the receiv-
ing end of the regime's displeasure: in 1966 and 1968, Sousa Tavares
endured spells in Caxias (a notorious jail for political prisoners),
a fact indirectly alluded to in the poem "Caxias 68," published in
Dual (1972). In 1970, one of Sophia's poetic anthologies would
run afoul of the censors for its unmistakable political tone. The
book's explosive title, *Grades* (Prison Bars), was recycled from the
third section of *Livro Sexto*; its subtitle was *Antologia de Poemas
de Resistência* (An Anthology of Resistance Poems). Undeterred,
she retaliated in her next collection, the aforementioned *Dual*, by
defiantly including some of the censored poems again. Ironically,
the regime seemed to take little notice of the contents of her latest
offering, no doubt because it had a much bigger crisis on its hands:
the 1972 publication of *New Portuguese Letters*, by Maria Isabel

Barreno, Maria Teresa Horta, and Maria Velho da Costa (The Three Marias). That book's banning immediately sparked an international outcry, uniting second-wave feminists across the world in a support campaign that generated a huge amount of adverse publicity for the regime.[5]

In the dying days of the dictatorship, 1973 saw the official re-opening of the Portuguese Writers Society, renamed the APE (the Portuguese Association of Writers), an event that had been in the planning since 1970. Sophia became president of its general assembly. In her opening speech, she said, "Escrever é exigir e não aceitar. . . . A poesia é necessariamente política" [To write is to demand, not to accept. . . . Poetry is necessarily political].[6] True to her words, Sophia would briefly take a seat as a socialist member of parliament in 1975. In the last three decades of her life, she continued to publish to great critical acclaim—and to speak against social injustice. She died in 2004, having lived long enough to rejoice at the independence of East Timor in a final tale, "O Anjo de Timor," published in 2003.

THE COLLECTION

The publication of *Contos Exemplares* in late 1962, a decade before the collapse of the regime, came at a turning point in the collective mood. According to the historian Filipe Ribeiro de Meneses, "if any year of the forty spent running his country tried Salazar's patience and desire to remain in power it was 1961" (2009: 610). The collection was dedicated to Sophia's husband: "Para o Francisco, que me ensinou a coragem e a alegria do combate desigual" [For Francisco, who taught me the courage and the joy of an unequal struggle]. The words *combate desigual* are an allusion to her husband's eponymous book, published in 1960. More broadly speaking, however, they align her with the struggle against an ideologically indefensible totalitarian regime, and may conceivably hint at a more literal combat—the war in progress in Angola.

The epigraph by Cervantes, author of *Novelas ejemplares* (*Exemplary Tales*), suggests that a didactic purpose, however indirect, lies beneath all the stories. In its definitive form, the collection is framed by "The Bishop's Dinner" and "The Three Kings," two pieces whose religious protagonists set moral examples, since they are ultimately presented as having the courage to follow their conscience. These tales are narrated from an omniscient perspective, as is the similarly allegorical "The Journey." By contrast, the remaining four stories, "The Portrait of Monica," "Beach," "Homer," and "The Man," deploy first-person narrators. While no less significant for their lessons, the mode of narration implies that these stories are inherently more subjective. "Homer" and "Beach" center on seemingly autobiographical recollections of formative moments: in childhood and early adulthood, respectively. Both take place by the beach, a liminal space between nature and culture. "The Portrait of Monica" and "The Man" are set in urban contexts and dated 1961 and 1959, respectively, which suggests that the narrative voice belongs to a rather more mature woman.

Although the title "Homer" is richly allusive, the story contains no apparent mention of the Greek poet. Instead, the narrator's fascination is focused on a character named Buzio, or Seashell, who lives on the fringes of society. Because readers are invited to see the tale as autobiographical from its opening statement ("When I was young"), it may profitably be interpreted in the context of what Sophia has described as a privileged moment of poetic initiation in her childhood: "I read [The Odyssey] when I was twelve years old and it was a revelation."[7] In a sense, this story conflates the monologues of the marginalized Buzio with a timeless classical tradition.

Buzio is the poet-prophet from whom the narrator learns an inaugural purity in communion with nature. Although he is regarded as a madman, his name aligns him with the natural world and he embodies a sort of primeval wisdom: "And his words drew together the dispersed fragments of the joy of the earth. He was invoking them, showing them, naming them: wind, freshness of the waters, gold of the sun, silence and brilliance of the stars." The words Buzio calls upon in a ritual of sacred invocation serve to connect the four elements: air, water, and fire all become integrated into "the joy of the earth."

The two urban tales further inscribe Sophia's resistance to dominant discourses. Both tackle the theme of contemporary social inequality through "exemplary" figures: one story concentrates on the upper echelons of society, while the other focuses on the underprivileged. "Portrait of Monica" (more accurately a caricature) damns with faint praise a character who renounces poetry, love, and holiness in a bid to secure an influential place in society. Monica's rejection of poetry stands in marked contrast to Sophia, who remained a committed poet until her death, while her daily negation of holiness reveals an alienation from core Christian values. The first-person narrator in "The Man," on the other hand, experiences a revelation when faced with an anonymous man who collapses in the street while carrying a child.

In this epiphany, the man with despair stamped on his face becomes a Christ-like figure, abandoned by his divine father in what also may be read as an allusion to Salazar's giving the lie to the ideology of "Deus, Pátria, Família" [God, Fatherland, Family]. Significantly, there is no resolution in this story. Though the man is taken off in an ambulance, the reader never learns precisely what becomes of him or of the innocent child. The narrator states that many years have elapsed since the events she witnessed took place: "The man, no doubt, is dead. But he continues at our side." This sentence not only brings the story into the present, it invites the reader into the scene by the use of "our." Considering that "The Man" was originally the closing tale in the collection and that, in this epilogue, the nameless man becomes interchangeable with the many "passing through the streets," the political imperative of "loving thy neighbor" would have been considerably heightened.

If hope for humankind is deferred in stories like "The Man" (or "The Journey," for that matter), it becomes the ultimate reward in "The Three Kings." Like "The Bishop's Dinner" and "The Man," the tale offers life-changing insights when privileged characters come face to face with indigent ones who bear the signs of hunger etched on their physiognomies. The Bishop (capitalized in the story itself) and each king in turn are ultimately transformed by their encounters with the material reality of the Other, which Emanuel Brandão relates to Levinas's ethics (2012: 47). In the Bishop's case, this involves him retracing his steps, after a betrayal comparable to that of Judas at the Last Supper. (In order to see the Christ-like figure again, the first-person narrator in "The Man" also decides to retrace her steps, even though she is powerless to affect his plight.)

In "The Bishop's Dinner," the poetic use of the fantastic or uncanny enables a discussion of pressing ethical issues. Sophia's retelling of a well-known Bible story in "The Three Kings" affords a similar opportunity. By vividly imagining the individual histories that led the three wise men to follow the star to Bethlehem, Sophia brings the subversive potential of Christianity to the fore. Although Balthazar in particular encounters the daily reality of human suffering in an imperfect world, all three kings choose the road less traveled. In the soaring and poetic finale, the star reveals to them, and by extension the reader, "joy, the wholeness of joy, without imperfection, the seamless vestments of joy, the immortal substance of joy." The repetition of the word links back to "Homer," where Buzio invokes "the joy of the Earth." Furthermore, the reiteration of "joy" enables Sophia (and her readers) to come full circle, to a dedication that foregrounded the "alegria do combate" [joy of combat].

While joy is featured at prominent points in the collection, hunger has a much stronger presence, and poverty truly becomes a leitmotif. On one level, the need for practicing Christians (the overwhelming majority of the Portuguese population) to respond to social injustice therefore constitutes a unifying thread. But it is my contention that the organic unity underlying these tales is furthermore filtered by the narrator's female gaze.

FEMALE CONSCIOUSNESS
IN A DIVIDED TIME

In 1962, when *Contos Exemplares* was first published, full political equality for Portuguese women was still more than a decade away. Until 1968, a married woman could not travel abroad without her husband's permission, nor did women have the same voting rights as men. Why then did Sophia not embrace feminist causes? Like most female activists of the time, she probably felt that conditions in Portugal were similarly untenable for the majority of men and women alike. Nonetheless, her gender unavoidably intervenes in the construction of poetic authority. Tellingly, an earlier poetry collection, *No Tempo Dividido*, contained the short poem "Santa Clara de Assis," which constructs the exceptional woman as a prophet(ess):

Eis aquela que parou em frente
Das altas noites puras e suspensas
Eis aquela que soube na paisagem
Adivinhar a unidade prometida:
Coração atento ao rosto das imagens,
Face erguida,
Vontade transparente
Inteira onde os outros se dividem. (1995, II:37)

Here is the one who stood still in front
Of deep pure suspended nights
Here is the one who managed to divine
In the landscape the promised unity:
Her heart attentive to the face of images,
Her head held high,
Her will transparent
Whole where others divide themselves.

Saint Clare of Assisi, in contrast to the odious Monica, is argu-
ably the image of what Sophia aspired to be: a visionary (female)
poet-prophet. And nowhere is this more obvious than in "Beach,"
the self-reflexive story that lies at the heart of the collection. In
this tale, the narrator registers multiple fragmentary impressions:
outside and inside; past, present, and future; dream and reality;
poverty and privilege; nature and society; the collective and the
personal. Since the time allusions in this tale stretch from the 1920s
to "the torments of the year 2000," the present evoked (1943) comes
across as being in flux.

It may be worth pointing out that, in 1943, Sophia had yet to
publish her first poetry collection. This fact might help explain
why the most memorable characters in "Beach" are male artists: a

nameless man, who moves in the same social circles as the narrator, and some shabby paid musicians, who do not. The nameless man is described as a visionary,[8] whose gaze glimpses something beyond everyday reality that can only be conveyed in verse. The verses cited, though unattributed, are Sophia's own and were subsequently included in a revised version of *No Tempo Dividido* (1995, II:11). The mysterious man then recites a few lines of poetry in English, pregnant with an elusive beauty. Although the provenance of his eerie verses is not identified, they are essentially nostalgic in tone.

A time of waiting (*espera*) lies at the heart of "Beach," in a kind of *mise en abyme*. In this context, it is surely not a coincidence that the narrator interjects a lengthy comment about the impoverished musicians: "They must have been either resigned or seething. I hope they were seething: that would have been less sad. A man in revolt, even if inglorious, is never completely defeated. But passive resignation, resignation through a progressive deafening of one's being, that is a complete failure and without cure." While the nameless man harks back to the past, the first-person narrator finds herself standing at a crossroads. She, like Gaspar in "The Three Kings," is willing to listen to the growth of time: "Solitude had created a transparent space of clarity around him . . . Gaspar thought: 'What could grow within time if not justice?'"

In "Beach," the oneiric atmosphere is abruptly curtailed when present-day reality intrudes with the news that Rommel, one of Hitler's generals, is retreating in the African desert. The narrator's reaction to this historical event, which can be dated to 1943, is unexpected: she intensely visualizes the soon-to-be-defeated men, as they carry on fighting, "knowing their cause unjust, their battle lost." This is as close as the collection gets to a comment on Portugal's colonial war in Africa: many Portuguese soldiers also would have been aware that they were fighting a lost cause. The use of the

Greek word for "men" at this juncture is striking, a defamiliarizing device, perhaps intended to draw attention to the essential inner core uniting humankind.

The story closes with the narrator and her friends on a balcony overlooking the sea, the scenery enveloped by fog. The blanket of mist means everything is shrouded in white, and neither moon nor stars can be seen. Earlier in the tale, there was a reference to Dom Sebastião, further underlining the ominous sense of waiting. Fernando Pessoa's celebrated 1934 collection, *Mensagem* (Message), ended with the poem "Fog" (2006: 182), which conjured precisely this sense of suspension. In a letter to her mother, probably written in the 1940s, Sophia included a copy of *Mensagem*, which she described as "um livro maravilhoso" [a wonderful book] (*Correspondência*, 2010: 33). She was particularly taken with "Horizonte" and "Monstrengo," two poems on the theme of daring to go beyond the world as it was known, of overcoming fear. Given this background, it is difficult not to read "Beach" as conveying a symbolic moment of uncertainty between past and future, both on an individual level and a collective one. While the point of no return is superficially related to 1943, it also extends to Portugal in the early 1960s, when the more mature Sophia was writing.

In "Beach," the narrator, like the inspired Saint Clare, "stood still in front / of deep pure suspended nights." Nonetheless, in the context of 1960s Portugal, as reflected in the fictional world of *Exemplary Tales*, the options for women remained severely limited. "The Bishop's Dinner" features kitchen-servants like Joana and Gertrude, along with the satellite women who revolve around the Lord of the Manor. Then there is the self-assured Monica, co-opted by a patriarchal system headed by the Prince of this World. But what about the nameless woman in "The Journey," an allegorical tale which—literally—ends on a cliffhanger? In the closing lines, as the woman clings to hope against the threat of annihilation, a leap of faith is required. While this scenario may offer a modern twist on Pascal's famous wager, it is the inner strength of this seemingly God-forsaken woman that ultimately may save her. Sophia mentioned in several interviews that she found writing this piece both terrifying and cathartic.[9] The woman's haunting determination may have reflected that of her creator, unwilling to be cowed by unequal struggles.

CONCLUSION

Contos Exemplares cleverly managed to expose the inner contradictions of Salazar's ideology of "Deus, Pátria, Família" in a way that generated a widespread following. That this collection remains relevant in our own turbulent times, more than fifty years after it was first published, is surely a sign of the power of Sophia's writing.

Clara Rocha rightly draws our attention to the presence of metatextual reflections on literature throughout the collection (2001: 83). It is worth stressing that these discussions (perhaps predictably, given the time frame) involved only learned *men*. To this day, some readers and critics still prefer to consider Sophia de Mello Breyner Andresen, one of the great women writers of twentieth-century Portugal, as a writer *tout court*. On closer inspection, however, "Beach" presciently articulated the fact that this gifted writer answered the call of 'destiny' in a way that was subliminally—if unavoidably—informed by her gender.[10] Unlike the melancholy nameless poet who stood, in that very same tale, "like a limit, like a boundary marker that said: 'From this point on the sea is no longer navigable,'" Sophia took it upon herself to navigate uncharted waters.

Today, across the Portuguese-speaking world, her poetic legacy continues to inspire generations of artists, female and male alike.[11] In short, her name has become synonymous with the Portuguese mother-tongue, alongside canonical predecessors such as Camões and Pessoa. She remains, however, one of the few pre-1974 women writers to have been enshrined by Portuguese literary history; as the exception that proves the rule, her consecration paradoxically serves to reinforce the unity of hegemonic cultural memory (Owen and Pazos Alonso 2011: 21). No wonder then that Sophia continues to be the stuff of legend.

NOTES

1. Given that the English-speaking environment is often less permeable to foreign literature, her inclusion in Helder Macedo and Ernesto Manuel de Melo e Castro's anthology, *Contemporary Portuguese Poets* (Carcanet New Press, 1978), was a decisive first step.

2. For further details about Delgado's challenge to Salazar, see Meneses 2009.

3. The manifesto is available on the very informative Biblioteca Nacional de Portugal site dedicated to Sophia, curated by her daughter Maria Andresen Sousa Tavares, who is an academic, along with a team of experts; http://purl.pt/19841/1/1960/1960-4.html.

4. For further details, please see Meneses (2009: 440–42). The contents of the letter to Salazar that sparked Dom António's political hounding can be viewed at http://www.fspes.pt/cartasalazar.html.

5. For further details about *New Portuguese Letters*, see the ongoing project, http://www.novascartasnovas.com/.

6. Her speech is available on the APE site, http://www.apescritores. pt/doc/Historia_APE.pdf. (See page 9.)

7. Zenith, 1997: 11. A much later poem, "Homer," clarifies the purity and harmony she associated with the Greek poet (1997: 110).

8. This character was probably modeled on Sophia's old friend José Zarco da Câmara (known as José Ribeira) since she states that he appeared in this particular short story (see her 1986 interview with Prado Coelho, republished in Amado and Morão, 2010: 176). The allusion in this tale may have been prompted by his death in May 1961 (see letter from Sophia to her mother, where she mourns his demise, published in Amado and Morão, 2010: 38).

9. See for instance the 1986 interview with Prado Coelho, republished in Amado and Morão (2010: 176).

10. As Anna Klobucka perceptively argues in a groundbreaking chapter devoted to Sophia's poetry, the gender markers that subtly inflect her writing have gone without comment for far too long. For instance, Klobucka examines how the complex intertextual dialogue that Sophia established with Pessoa is heavily gendered (2009: 183–199). In a prose context, "O Silêncio," a female-centered short story composed in 1966 but not published until 1984 in *Histórias da Terra e do Mar*, would also warrant closer gender analysis. It could be profitably juxtaposed with a tale like Clarice Lispector's "Love," from the collection *Family Ties*.

11. One recent example is the Mozambican writer Mia Couto, who used excerpts of Sophia's poetry as epigraphs for several chapters of his bestselling 2009 novel *Jesusalém* (translated as *The Tuner of Silences* by David Brookshaw, 2013).

BIBLIOGRAPHY

Primary Sources

Andresen, Sophia de Mello Breyner. *Contos Exemplares*, eighth ed. Lisbon: Portugália, n.d. [first ed. 1962].

———. *Correspondência 1959–1978*. Lisbon: Guerra & Paz, 2010.

———. *Grades* [Antologia de Poemas de Resistência]. Lisbon: Publicações Dom Quixote, 1970.

————. Interview with Eduardo Prado Coelho. *Revista do ICALP* 6 (1986): 60–77. Republished in Maria Teresa Amado and Paula Morão, *Sophia de Mello Breyner Andresen: Uma Vida de Poeta. Fotobiografia.* Lisbon: Caminho, 2010.

————. *Obra Poética*, second ed., vols. I–III. Lisbon: Caminho, 1995–96.

————. "Os Três Reis do Oriente." Lisbon: Estúdios Cor, 1965.

Translations into English

Andresen, Sophia de Mello Breyner. *Log Book: Selected Poems*, trans. by Richard Zenith. Manchester: Carcanet, 1997.

————. *Marine Rose: Selected Poems*, trans. by Ruth Fainlight. Reading Ridge, Conn.: Black Swann, 1988.

————. *Shores, Horizons, Voyages: Selected Poems*, trans. by Rui Cascais Parada. Hong Kong: Orchid, 2005.

Secondary Sources

Amado, Maria Teresa, and Paula Morão. *Sophia de Mello Breyner Andresen: Uma Vida de Poeta. Fotobiografia.* Lisbon: Caminho, 2010.

Brandão, Emanuel. *Poesia e Limite: Uma Leitura Teológica da Obra de Sophia de Mello Breyner.* Leça da Palmeira: Letras e Coisas, 2012.

Castro, Pedro Jorge. "Um casal apaixonado contra Salazar." *Sábado*, 11 April 2014, accessed online at http://www.sabado.pt/.

Klobucka, Anna. *O Formato Mulher: A emergência da autoria feminina na poesia portuguesa.* Coimbra: Angelus Novus, 2009.

Meneses, Filipe Ribeiro de. *Salazar: A Political Biography* (New York: Enigma Books 2009).

Owen, Hilary, and Cláudia Pazos Alonso. *Antigone's Daughters? Gender, Genealogy, and the Politics of Authorship in 20th-Century Portuguese Women's Writing.* Lewisburg, Penn.: Bucknell University Press, 2011.

Pessoa, Fernando. *A Little Larger than the Entire Universe*, trans. by Richard Zenith. London: Penguin, 2006.

Rocha, Clara. "Para uma Leitura dos 'Contos Exemplares.'" *Máthesis* 10 (2001): 73–84.

Zenith, Richard, "Foreword" to *Log Book: Selected Poems by Sophia de Mello Breyner*. Manchester: Carcanet Press, 1997.

————. "In the Name of Things," 31 March 2004; accessed online at http://www.poetryinternationalweb.net/pi/site/cou_article/item /4628/In-the-Name-of-Things.

Online Resources (in Portuguese)

"Retrato de Monica," audio and text; http://cvc.instituto-camoes.pt /contomes/19/texto.html.

"Sophia de Mello Breyner Andresen," edited by Maria Andresen Sousa Tavares; web design by Cecilia Matos; http://purl.pt/19841/1/. Lisbon: BNP, 2011.

exemplary tales

one

— ❧ —

THE BISHOP'S

DINNER

I

The house was large, white, and very old. In front there was a square
courtyard. To the right there was an orange grove where day and
night a fountain flowed. To the left there was a box-tree garden,
humid and shady, with its camellias and its tiled benches.

In the middle of the facade there was a granite staircase covered
in moss. Opposite the steps, on the other side of the courtyard, was
the large gate that led to the street.

The back of the house faced west. And from its windows opening
onto orchards and fields one could see the river flowing through the
green flatlands and in the distance one could make out blue hills
whose summits, on certain afternoons, turned purple.

On the slopes carved into terraces grew the vineyard. It was there
on the poor soil that good wine was born. The poorer the soil, the
richer the wine. Wine in which, as in a poem, are hidden the flavors
of flowers and of earth, the ice of winter, the sweetness of spring,
and the fire of summer. And it was said that the wine from those
slopes, like a good poem, never went bad with age. To the right,
between the flatlands and the hills, grew the woods, woods laden
with murmurs and fragrances and which in the fall turned golden.

But now it was winter, a hard winter, desolate and cold, and the wind was unraveling the blue smoke rising from the small, poor houses. The roads were covered in mud. A prolonged sobbing seemed to flow through the country lanes.

The Lord of the Manor was standing, leaning against the lit fireplace in the main hall, surrounded by guests, mostly cousins, and a few neighbors. He was silent, removed from the conversation: he was pondering, weighing his arguments, defending before himself his cause and its justice. Only the last guest was missing and that was the Bishop.

The Lord of the Manor had a favor to ask of the Bishop. It was for this very reason that he was inviting him to dinner. And that is why, while awaiting his arrival, he pondered and prepared the arguments justifying his cause.

In fact, there, in those peaceful lands, in those submissive domains where he and his father and his grandfathers had exercised undisputed authority, there where order had reigned forever, a seed of warfare had now arisen.

This seed of warfare was the new priest, a young priest with a torn cassock and unruly hair, the parish priest from Varzim, a miserable little village where the tillers of the vineyards lived. For a long time Varzim had been poor and always growing poorer, and for a long time the parish priests of Varzim had accepted with patience, always with more patience, the poverty of their parishioners. But this new priest was speaking of a justice which wasn't the justice of the Lord of the Manor. And it seemed to the Lord of the Manor that, day by day, week by week, month by month, his presence was growing like an accusation accusing him, like a finger pointing, like a flaming sword touching him. And there in his house whose masters had been from generation to generation symbols of honor, virtue, order, and justice, it seemed to him now that every gesture of the Priest of Varzim was calling him to judgment to answer for the consumptives spitting blood, for the old with no means of support, for the stunted children, for the madmen, the blind, and the lame begging alms on the streets.

Finally there had arisen a question of accounts with a tenant and the Abbé of Varzim had defended the tenant.

"Father," the Lord of the Manor had said, "I thought your job was to attend to prayers, not to accounts. Moral problems are your concern. Practical problems are my concern. I beg you to allow Caesar to concern himself with what is Caesar's. I do not give orders in your church: I only attend and support it. The problem we are discussing is mine, it is of the world, it is a material and practical problem."

"Of our own hunger," answered the Priest of Varzim, "we can say that it is a material and practical problem. The hunger of others is a moral problem."

And the issue continued. It grew from day to day. The Lord of the Manor was old and accustomed to his possessions and to giving orders. His conveniences, his commodities, his advantages and his interests all seemed to him absolute ethical rights, sacred principles of peace and order. That is why he had invited the Bishop to dinner. To make clear to him the justice of his cause. But it was hard for him to accuse his adversary. The Priest of Varzim lived in poverty and chastity. No one could say he was not a good priest. His piety was visible and the fame of his charity flowed from mouth to mouth along the terraced mountainsides. He sat at the table with consumptives in their rags filthy with blood and entered the dwelling place of the leper. He gave, it was said, all that he had and received in his house homeless wanderers. Day after day, that face sculpted by harsh daily sacrifice, that gaze pierced by a vision of suffering, those narrow shoulders, those clothes faded by sun and rain, those ragged boots on all the roads, seemed to be turning into an image of the poverty and misery of Varzim.

In a certain way, the Lord of the Manor felt irritated by the insignificance of that adversary. He wasn't used to fighting, he was used to giving orders. Others had fought for him and had won. But, since he himself had now to fight, he would have at least preferred to fight with a strong and powerful man like himself. An adversary so thin and helpless made him ashamed.

At first he had interpreted the attitude of the Abbé of Varzim as being an expression of social revolt from an offspring of the poor.

But then he came to discover that the priest was a distant relative of his own distant relatives and that the hunger written on his face was not hereditary, but in fact voluntary. He had rejected his place among the rich and taken his place among the poor. This news did not bring rapture to the Lord of the Manor.

For he was used to saying: "All power comes from God." And he thought that for that reason a priest ought to respect all established power and respect money and social standing, all expressions of power. And he considered it quite unacceptable for a man to reject the legacy of his parents in order to align himself on the side of the impoverished. A man of good family going into the priesthood ought to become a Bishop, a Nuncio, or even a Pope. At least a Monsignor. Never the parish priest of a village in the mountains.

The attitude of the new priest shocked him, like a kind of treason.

Adding to all of this, the Lord of the Manor, a great gourmet, knowledgeable about wines and a bon vivant, detested ascetics, who seemed to him to be insane, pretentious, and dangerous, scarcely human and always desiring something unnatural. Now he heard that the chickens, nuts, grapes, and pears that he was accustomed to sending to the successive priests of Varzim on a regular basis, were no longer arriving at their destination, which was the priest's dinner table, but were being distributed throughout the famine of Varzim. He also had heard that the priest was giving away the cabbage from his garden and the grapes from his vines. He even was giving away the milk from his goat. He was giving away everything. That's why he walked around like a famished person himself, with his worn-out cassock and his shameful boots.

This was going against common usage, against custom. This was no longer virtue: this was disorder, abnormality, Bolshevism.

But the worst thing of all was the Sunday Mass. The Lord of the Manor had always attended in a distracted way Sunday sermons in Varzim. They were sermons that spoke of patience, resignation, and hope in a better world. Sermons that didn't seem to apply to him. In a way, for him no world could be better, and for this reason he wished to go to heaven as late as possible. As a result, while the preachers spoke, everything distracted him. The painting on the ceiling distracted him, the crying child distracted him. And so he would go on to remembering something about sulfites or the grape harvest or the sale of his wine. He would think about his business dealings.

But now his mind couldn't wander. Now the new priest spoke of charity. And the charity of which he spoke was not the well-known and peaceful practice of the usual apportioning out of alms. It was a commandment of a solemn and demanding God, a naked word of God piercing the spirit of man.

All this disturbed and troubled the Lord of the Manor. Home from Mass, he dined badly. Theology wasn't his specialty and this new commandment of charity seemed to him to be the result of the new and dangerous ideas of our era. He had a firm and unquestioning faith, based not on the Gospels, which he had never read, but rather on his good manners and his respect for the established way of things. He would give alms to the poor on Saturday and go to Mass on Sunday. He had a special bench in church and he never arrived late. And he kept up in his house the ancient custom of always maintaining in his kitchen a table for the poor. At any time of day, a meal was served to any beggar who knocked on the door. Of course, to take advantage of that beneficence the beggar had to be from another region or, being from around there, he would have to be recognized as truly poverty-stricken. Truly poverty-stricken, around there, were Lucio, who had no legs, Manuel, who had no arms, Quintino, who was blind, Deaf Joana, who was a widow and a hundred years old, and Maria the Mad. Those were truly poor: after all, none of them could work. But Pedro da Serra who had nine children and earned about fifteen cents a day digging gravel, he wasn't truly poor since he had a salary and two arms.

The table of the poor was a special table. For reasons of hierarchy and for reasons of hygiene: one couldn't impose on one's servants any contact with mud, dust, filth, bad smells, and the illnesses of the poor. As a result, in the ordering of that little world of which the Lord of the Manor was the head, the impoverished also had their place just a bit below that of the servants, a bit above that of the dogs. But in spite of everything it was a good place. Next to the bread and the wine, in front of the plate of soup, the cook had orders to always place a small coin.

And that's the way traditions were maintained in that house. That house so beautiful, with its clean lines, with its materials, both lofty and base, with its crumbling walls, its old tiles and its great bright and straight facade, whose beauty lay just in the perfect balance of its spaces and its volumes and in the nakedness of the whitewash and the stone.

But inside, something was disturbing that harmony. Pompous furniture, false and gilded, had been added to the dark old furniture. A strange feeling of the nouveau riche was slowly impregnating the ancient, simple, and austere nobility. An excess of carpets was hiding the sweet wood of the floors. Complicated curtains were detracting from the cold brightness of the tiles and the pure whiteness of the walls.

But above all—oh, above all else—the portraits of the Master and Mistress of the Manor, rosy and stylized, seated in great elaborate armchairs, beside a large Chinese vase, contrasted bitterly with the dry and sober portraits of their ancestors. But the Lord of the Manor didn't notice this contrast and enjoyed seeing himself, rosy as a ham, and with his hands tapered to a miracle, there beside his grandparents. There they were, almost all of them: the one who was wounded in five battles, the one who had sailed to the ends of the earth and died of scurvy, the one who was shipwrecked off India, the one who was denounced and tortured, the one who died in prison, the one who died in exile. There they were, almost all of them: the one who had lost an eye in Ceuta, the one who had lost an arm in Diu (Portuguese India), the one who had lost his head to King Phillip in the War of Restoration. There they were, almost all of them, in their sober portraits, beside the Lord of the Manor, who had never lost a thing.

And when the Lord of the Manor passed before the portraits with visitors he would explain:

"It is customary in my family that each new generation leaves its portrait here. That is why mine is already here. I like maintaining traditions."

These exhibits of portraits deeply amused a distant relative of the Lord of the Manor whom everyone in the family called Cousin Pedro.

This Cousin Pedro was the most legitimate representative of nobility in the region and the most fallen away. His grandfather, his father, and he himself had slowly sold houses, fields, and farms to the grandfather and father of the Lord of the Manor. And the portraits exhibited there had also changed ownership, along with the houses and the farms. The portraits, however, as well as changing their owners, had also changed their line of descent.

But Cousin Pedro didn't need the portraits: he himself, with his austere and dry air, was equal to any portrait. In this he contrasted sharply with the Lord of the Manor, who was swarthy, corpulent, and florid, with coarse hands and short, avid fingers.

The ruin of men like Cousin Pedro, his father, and his grandfather always seemed a bit inexplicable. They didn't merely squander their possessions, but also their talents. Their qualities didn't find their way to fulfillment. It was as if the relationship between them and life had been broken. To what were their days, their spirit, their courage dedicated? What renunciation was driving them? What failure was dominating them?

Cousin Pedro had a defined sensibility like that of an artist, he had the intelligence of an inventor and the spirit of justice of a revolutionary. But all his life long he had never done a thing. Was it his fault or could it be the fault of the circles in which he moved? Could it be because the image of the Lord of the Manor, the images of the numerous lords of the manor, made him draw back with nausea before all those victories? Or could he be a spirit woven of disillusion, doubt, and irony? Or could it be that his rejection signified a will to divestiture, an almost metaphysical renunciation?

The Lord of the Manor didn't worry about these problems, which in any case were no concern of his: for him, those relatives of his were merely decorative failures, likeable and well-mannered. He valued himself and his own family much more, they were people capable of preserving and adding to their fortune and their position in life.

In fact, the grandfather of the Lord of the Manor had married the daughter of a slave-dealer and his father the daughter of a money-lender. From that there had come a great increase in the family wealth, wealth that now allowed the Lord of the Manor to maintain close relations with powerful financial figures and play a role on various administrative boards. While all this was happening, Cousin Pedro's grandfather had married, scandalizing the entire region, an actress of the Romantic era, and his father had married a relative as ruined as he himself. As for Cousin Pedro, he hadn't gotten married at all. Tall and thin, he would walk alone through the countryside and the twilit shadows.

But in spite of all this, the Lord of the Manor took great pleasure in this relationship which proved his good ancestry. Having Cousin Pedro to dinner made him feel as if he had one of the personages from the gallery of portraits seated at his table.

However, today he had not invited him. For Cousin Pedro had subversive ideas: he defended democracy, freedom of the press, the right to strike, and was used to quoting the catechism, saying that to not pay a just salary to a worker is a sin that cries out to heaven. This led the Lord of the Manor to suspect that he was a Communist. And it also led him to realize that it wouldn't be appropriate to invite him to dinner with the Bishop: in fact it was obvious that Cousin Pedro would have defended the Priest of Varzim.

So, the Lord of the Manor, with his practical sense, so perfect it was almost sinister, had organized that gathering with all prudence: he had only invited discreet and safe people, whose support, agreement, and silence he could entirely rely upon.

Now it was already past eight: rain beat musically against the windows, but inside the room light and warmth reigned.

And standing among his innocuous guests, removed from the conversations, leaning against the stonework of the fireplace, in which the twisted stump of a vine slowly burned, the Lord of the

Manor was thinking about the real purpose of that dinner: to ask the Bishop to transfer the priest from Varzim to another district. He was thinking over his words and weighing his arguments. He didn't want his request to seem mean-spirited or vengeful.

He wanted to explain with clarity that the new priest was a danger to the social order, the very order that he, owner of the fields, the orchards, the pine groves, and the vineyards, in the midst of his well-pruned garden, well planted and well swept, in the midst of his old house, well kept, nicely whitewashed and nicely waxed, in the midst of his inherited silverware and purchased silverware, in the midst of his old furniture and new carpets, that he himself stood for.

But—in spite of such powerful arguments—the request was difficult to make.

Meanwhile, in his car, the Bishop was coming along the road. His headlights lit up hillsides, footpaths, thickets, lowly huts, and, every so often, distant farm gates.

In the sky covered with heavy rain clouds not a single star could be seen. It was a night of total darkness. Sometimes the car would slide in the mud of the road.

An unruly wind was shaking the branches of the trees and the thoughts of the Bishop were crisscrossing in his head.

To ask for something is a difficult thing. And all the more difficult when the one from whom you are asking is rich and powerful. But from whom could he ask if not the rich and powerful?

In fact, the Bishop had a request to make of the Lord of the Manor. That was the real reason he had accepted the invitation.

The roof of the most beautiful church in his diocese was falling to ruin. It was a church dating from the seventeenth century, famous throughout the region, and it had been ordered built precisely by an ancestor of the Lord of the Manor. For in ancient times, when a powerful man found himself ill or with a heavy conscience, he would promise to have a church built to bring peace to his body and soul. But nowadays there were medicines for all illnesses and arguments for all consciences. Nowadays "rich men" no longer ordered churches to be built in honor of Our Lady of Hope. Nowadays sickness was no longer the same for the rich and the poor. Nowadays with diet, analysis, X-rays, clinics, sleep and vitamin regimes, a rich man's health was almost guaranteed. And nowadays bourgeois certitudes had swept anxiety away and had made hope unnecessary.

As a result, it was in vain that the Bishop had made a list of the eminent personalities of the city. The piety of the faithful did not rise as high as the roof. The results of his petitioning had scarcely provided enough to restore the main altar. And the Church of Our Lady of Hope remained in ruins.

And that is how the Bishop had resolved to turn to the Lord of the Manor to ask him for the one hundred thousand escudos needed to fix the roof. But it was hard for him to have to ask for so much money. It was true that the Lord of the Manor was a virtuous man. But who can trust in the generosity of a virtuous man? Virtuous men are reasonable and prudent, and generosity, being the virtue of those who give precisely what they can't afford to give, is by its very nature an unreasonable thing, contrary to the habits of prudent men. Only saints and madmen are generous. That is why the Bishop, as the night flowed along beside him, slowly shook his head, dubious about the outcome of his request.

He remembered, however, that the Lord of the Manor, being, like the Pharisees of old, a man of official virtue, must also be a vain man. For his long experience had taught him that virtuous men are usually of an extreme vanity. They carefully cultivate their good repute, wishing it splendor and fame. And without doubt the Lord of the Manor, so jealous of the traditions of his family, would not be indifferent to the fact that the Church of Our Lady of Hope— now in ruins—had three centuries ago been constructed by one of his ancestors. Perhaps the vanity of the Lord of the Manor would mean a roof for the church.

The Bishop was old and tired with the world. And as the head-lights illuminated the curves of the hillside, he thought: "How sad it is to have to rely on the vanity of men." And suddenly he felt like not making his request.

But the Devil, spying on events, decided to interfere.

A few moments later the Bishop arrived at the house. His auto-mobile passed through the gate and its lights shone directly on the beautiful granite staircase. The car did a U-turn and the headlights ran the length of the white facade, etching out the shape of the windows.

And once again the Bishop's heart was moved before the pure and antique beauty of the walls and the stone.

It was raining. A servant came down with an umbrella. The Bishop got out of the car and, slowly, heavily, his hand supported by the moss-covered granite balustrade, climbed the stairway and went into the warm and brightly lit interior.

The Lord and Lady of the Manor were already awaiting him in the great empty entrance hall, where blue tiles told, in numerous realistic details, stories of idyllic unreal hunts, with hunters and deer, thickets and birds. After the customary greetings, the three went toward the large living room. The visitors had interrupted their conversations and had gotten to their feet to come and speak to the Bishop.

But no sooner were the greetings concluded than the sound of a great crash was heard from outside.

There was a small moment of confusion. People ran to the windows and they saw in the well-lit courtyard a large automobile, black and sumptuous, that had smashed into the left-hand pillar of the entrance gate.

This caused a great sensation. There were exclamations and questions. Everyone assumed that the car had skidded on the mud and everyone was saying:

"We have to see if anyone is hurt."

But the front door of the car opened and out came the chauffeur to open the rear door.

And from the rear door there emerged a tall, straight man, in a dark overcoat, a hat with its brim turned down, and the face of an important person.

It was raining harder than ever, but the man, with neither haste nor delay, looked straight ahead and crossed the courtyard deliberately, as if the rain were not making him wet.

But already the servant with the umbrella was descending the stairs at a run and already the Lord of the Manor was rushing toward the entrance hall.

As soon as the features of the unknown figure came clear in the light from the door, the Lord of the Manor's arm made a large gesture of welcome.

The unknown man said his name. A name that was heard with pleasure. It was the name of a highly important man.

"My car skidded on the street," said the Highly Important Man, "and crashed into your gate."

The Lord of the Manor gave immediate orders for the accident to be attended to. He ordered the car to be brought inside the courtyard and he ordered that they telephone a garage in the nearby city so they could send a mechanic to repair the damage. But the city was more than half an hour away. As a result, the Highly Important Man was invited to join the dinner.

The new guest quickly made a good impression on everyone. He was dark-visaged, tall, rather thin than fat. He had that indeterminate age of businessmen who are at the height of their careers. He wasn't old, but he seemed never to have been young.

"He's very nice," murmured Cousin Ana to Cousin Mariana.

"Very nice, indeed," answered Cousin Mariana.

Only the son of the Lord of the Manor didn't like the new guest. He noticed that the shadow of that man was enormous and covered the ceiling, gesturing like a huge octopus. But that was something only the child had seen.

And when the Highly Important Man asked him his name, he answered in all seriousness:

"My name is John."

And later he asked:

"Why is it that your shadow is so big?"

The guest did not answer the child's question. He laughed and asked:

"How old are you?"

"Nine."

"You are still very young."

John continued to stare at the immense shadow on the ceiling. Then he looked at the man again and said:

"I don't like you."

The guest laughed once again and responded:

"You are still very young. When you grow up perhaps you will be my friend."

The presence of the Highly Important Man brought a great liveliness to the dinner. He was the center of attention and of conversation and his sensible opinions made the best of impressions. And when, toward the end of dinner, the conversation focused on the problems of these times, everyone listened to him with bated breath.

"These times," said the Important Man "are a time of crisis: we are dominated by materialism. Even in the fields, where spirituality ought to reign, we hear constant talk about material problems. Shakespeare, Camões, Dante spoke of the problems of the human soul. Today poets discuss workers' salaries and living standards in various countries. But man is not merely matter: he is also spirit. However, our times only see material problems. It is a time of revolt. Men don't want to accept things. Patience and resignation are words that have lost their meaning. The man of these times wants the kingdom of God to be here on this earth. It is the sin of revolt. Now it is a serious matter that this spirit grows present in art, in literature, in science, in philosophy, and in the newspapers. But most serious of all, that which is truly a cause for scandal, is to see that the spirit of materialism and of revolt is insinuating itself not just among Catholics, but even among priests themselves."

"The church," the Bishop interrupted, "cannot ignore social problems."

"I agree. I agree," continued the Important Man. "I know the doctrine of the church very well. The church is in this world and cannot ignore the world. But the mission of the church is transcendent: its duty is to guide man to his eternal destiny. 'Render unto Caesar the things which are Caesar's; and unto God the things that are God's'—those were the words of Christ in an occupied country. It isn't the task of the Church to commit itself to the solution of material problems, a solution that in any case is always imperfect, transitory, and dubious."

"The commandment for charity is very clear," said the Bishop.

"But it can be interpreted in many ways," continued the Important Man. "And I think many today interpret it badly: the charity they know is only material. They would say that man lives by bread alone. Look at what happened with the worker priests. But, without going so far off, we can already see among us Christians and even priests who speak like Communists."

"That's true!" interrupted the Lord of the Manor, remembering the Abbé of Varzim and rejoicing in the direction the conversation had taken.

But the Important Man was already going on with his discourse:

"Our era only puts its hope in the solution of material problems. A poor hope. Today I saw a spectacle that filled me with sorrow. A symbolic spectacle. I passed by a church that is called Our Lady of Hope. It is a lovely work of the seventeenth century. But it is in ruins. The Catholics of today discuss the problems of housing, but allow the very house of God to fall into decay. This, Reverend Bishop, I saw today in your diocese."

The Bishop blushed as if with guilt and answered:

"It is true, it is true. The Church of Our Lady of Hope is in ruins. Believe me, that is one of my greatest concerns. I have to arrange some solution. But for that I will have to count on the help of those who can truly help me."

"Indeed, indeed," said the Important Man. "We must at all cost preserve the legacy of the past. Disorder reigns in the world. But here, in our country, order still manages to conquer disorder."

"That's really true!" said Cousin Conceiçao.

Cousin Conceiçao was seated at the side of the Important Man. She was amazed. Her heart welcomed with enthusiasm every word that he said. She was sixty years old, a widow and the greatest landowner in the region. Her piety had a combative character, but her true gospel was the *Daily News*. She had no children and she was the official organizer of charity festivals. Her name appeared at the top of all the lists of benevolent associations. And she was the president of the knitting project. Once a week the benefactors of that project would meet in Cousin Conceiçao's house and, while they gossiped and knitted for the poor, the afternoon would gently flow by, interrupted only by a tea time so abundantly supplied that it would have served to feed the nine starving children of Pedro da Serra for a week.

Cousin Conceiçao began to explain to the Important Man the transcendent work of the knitting project. The Important Man approved. The conversation was agreeable.

The Lord of the Manor was feeling quite happy. The conversation of the new guest was fitting so well with his own purposes.

The words he had said were exactly the words he needed to hear at that moment; now he felt no hesitation, no doubts, no scruples. Now his decision was made: he would ask the Bishop at the end of the dinner to transfer the Abbé of Varzim to another parish.

And, content, his soul at peace, his mind free of uncertainty, he looked happily around him.

The vine trunk was burning in the fireplace, the electric lights fixed on the picture frames illumined the pheasants, the grapes, and the lemons of the still lifes, the candles shone on the table and the shadows coiled in the high corners of the ceiling. The Lord of the Manor liked being seated at his table with guests. Nothing pleased him more than giving food to those who were not hungry. He felt as if he were reigning over the chinaware and over the guests. And he had never felt as happy as on that day. Solid was the weight of the silverware. Solid was his kingdom. The Abbé of Varzim was a poor shadow, a ghost lost among beggars and crags, unreal and abstract like an idea that isn't of this world.

The dinner was reaching its end. The conversation was now

general and had risen a half note. The servants were scurrying around the table.

A bit giddy from the rapidity of the words, the Bishop looked at the shadows on the ceiling. Then, he lowered his gaze and saw before him the bread and the wine placed on the table.

Following the dinner, the Lord of the Manor led the Bishop and the Important Man to a small room, where the three sat down and had coffee.

The Important Man spoke once again of the Church of Our Lady of Hope. The Bishop told how the church had been constructed by an ancestor of the Lord of the Manor and explained the problem of the roof. The Important Man immediately offered fifty thousand escudos and the Lord of the Manor offered another fifty thousand. Then the Lord of the Manor explained to the Bishop the problem of the Priest of Varzim. The Man of Importance supported the arguments of the Lord of the Manor. The Bishop agreed that the attitude of the new priest to the question of the tenant was imprudent. The Lord of the Manor continued his complaint and the Important Man continued his argument. The Bishop promised that he would transfer the parish priest to another place.

The Lord of the Manor handed over a check and the Important Man handed over another check.

The Abbé of Varzim had been sold for a rooftop.

No one spoke of an exchange or a sale. No one used any shocking words. But when the three stood up and walked back toward the other guests in the great hall, the spirit of the Bishop was heavy with confusion. He was like a man who, involved in a business he doesn't really understand and convinced by a smooth-talking lawyer, buys something he doesn't want to buy and sells something he doesn't want to sell.

And God in heaven had pity on that Bishop because he was lost and alone and didn't know how to combat the subtle discourse of the Lords of this World.

II

A clock on the wall struck ten and a beggar knocked twice on the kitchen door.

It was the cook Gertrude who opened the door. She looked at the man without enthusiasm. She didn't know him, but it wasn't necessary to ask who he was: he was just another beggar.

The cook felt like telling him to come back later. The dinner had given her a lot of work and she still had to wash the dishes and straighten out the kitchen. But she had orders to give food to any poor person who knocked on the door while there was a light on in the house.

Therefore she said:

"Come in."

And added:

"Don't get the floor dirty."

A request impossible to satisfy. The soaked rags of the beggar were dripping with rain. There on the tiled floor, his naked feet were wet and covered with mud.

"Good evening," said the man.

"Good evening," answered Joana, the old servant.

Joana was seated beside the fire. She had a black shawl across her back and her eyes were of a colorless blue, as if faded by time.

Gertrude made no response to the good evenings. She gazed conspicuously at the water dripping from the beggar's rags.

"Come and get dry here beside the fire," said Joana.

Angry, Gertrude turned to the old servant.

"Don't you see that he's going to make a mess of the whole kitchen, that he's going to cover the floor with muddy footsteps?"

Then she turned to the man, pointed with her finger at the bench in front of the stone table for the poor and said:

"Your place is over there."

The man went toward the place the cook had pointed to. Each of his steps left behind an imprint on the tiled floor.

Gertrude kept a careful eye on the cutlery and on the silver serving plates piled on the table of rose-colored stone. Then, noting that there was a sufficient distance between the beggar and the plates, she said:

"Sit down."

The man sat down and she added:

"I'll heat you some soup."

She took a large pot standing to the side and placed it over a burner on the stove.

After that, she cut a piece of bread, filled a cup with wine, and put the bread and wine in front of the man.

Then he said:

"I have to speak with the Lord of the Manor."

"Alms are on Saturday," Gertrude answered.

"But I have to speak to the Lord of the Manor today," the man responded.

"Today isn't Saturday. And besides not being Saturday, it's late. And besides being late, we have visitors. Today we have the Bishop here and besides the Bishop we have a man even more important than the Bishop."

"But I have to speak to the Lord of the Manor tonight. It's important."

"Important things are for important people," answered Gertrude.

"Don't be a fool, man. You want the Lord of the Manor to come here, now, to speak to you? Don't even think of it!"

Outside the storm seemed to grow stronger.

The door from the corridor opened and a servant and a maid entered. The servant was carrying a tray with coffee cups, the maid a tray with wineglasses.

"Good evening," said the man.

"Good evening," they responded.

They put down the trays and the cook began immediately to wash the wineglasses.

"Well," said the servant, looking at the poor man, "we have lots of visitors today. Visitors in the great hall and visitors in the kitchen."

The man stood up, took a step toward the servant and said:

"Listen . . ."

"Don't take another step," interrupted the cook. "Look at how you're messing up my whole kitchen."

The man stayed where he was. But, turning to the servant, he went on:

"Listen, please, listen! I have to speak to the Lord of the Manor. Go to the dining hall and ask him to come here."

"I've already told him," explained Gertrude to the servant, "that today isn't Saturday and that we have visitors. But he doesn't understand something that simple."

"Fella," said the servant, approaching the poor man, "have you ever seen a gentleman leave his visitors in the dining hall to come to the kitchen to talk to a beggar? Calm down, take it easy, it can't happen. That's what the world is like. We have to be patient."

The man turned to the maid and begged:

"Listen, I beg of you: go upstairs and tell the Lord of the Manor that I need to talk to him this very day."

"I have orders to never go and bring messages to the hall when there are visitors. Everything has its proper place."

Far off, there was the roll of thunder.

Gertrude took a soup plate from the cupboard, dipped the ladle in the pot, put the soup in the plate.

Then she approached the table of the poor, put down the plate, and said to the man:

"Sit down and eat."

The man sat down with a tired look, but did not begin to eat.

The door from the corridor opened once again and one of the chambermaids came in.

She was in a bad mood.

The man said:

"Good evening."

She looked at him with disdain and asked the serving maid:

"Where did you put the keys to the clothing closet?"

"They're in the ironing room," answered the other maid.

The chambermaid sighed, sat down on a bench, and grumbled:

"Even at this hour more work comes my way."

"What's happened then?" asked the cook.

"What's happened is they've invited the new guest, the Most Important Gentleman, to sleep here. And at this hour of the night I still have to go straighten out the room and make the bed."

"He must really be an important person," Gertrude remarked.

"It's obvious that he is," said the chambermaid. "When he talks, it's as if he is the lord of everything."

"Listen, please," said the poor man, getting up and taking a step in the direction of the chambermaid.

But the cook interrupted him once again.

"Stay where you are, don't make my kitchen even dirtier."

Then she turned to the chambermaid and once again explained:

"He wants to talk, today, now, to the Lord of the Manor. I've already told him its impossible, but he doesn't understand."

"Listen!" said the man, turning to the chambermaid. "Listen, I beg of you: go yourself to get the Lord of the Manor."

"I'm a chambermaid. I haven't been told to deliver messages up in the hall. That's not my task."

The thunderstorm now seemed close by. A lightning flash turned the windows blue and a thunderclap could be heard off toward the mountains. Everyone made the sign of the cross.

"Oh, the poor!" said old Joana from her spot. "There's always a reason for saying no to them. The poor are hungry and cold but most of all they are alone. If I were young I would go up to ask for you. But I am old and can't climb the stairs anymore."

"If you did get up there no one would pay you any notice," said Gertrude sternly.

And turning to the man she went on:

"Give up asking. You can see already no one's going to pay attention."

Another flash of lightning revealed the garden outside livid and transfigured and then a peal of thunder was heard, shaking the house to its very foundations.

The electric lights went out. The servants crossed themselves in the dark where only the embers from the fire were glowing.

Quickly, Gertrude struck a match and lit two candles.

"Give me one of them," said the servant, "I have to go right up to light the candles."

The cook gave him one of the candles and the servant left, followed by the serving maid and the chambermaid.

Gertrude took from a cupboard a small candlestick on which she stuck the candle. Then she placed the candlestick on top of the large table in the middle of the kitchen.

Rain was beating desperately against the windows. The thunderstorm was growing more and more violent. The countryside, blue and blasted by lightning, rose up in the windows and then quickly disappeared, submerged in the darkness. The rolling of thunder was awakening an immensity.

"Protect us, Saint Barbara!" said old Joana. "The storm is right on top of us."

Gertrude opened a drawer.

"What are you looking for?" asked the old one.

"I'm going to burn rosemary. They say it helps," answered the cook.

And she took from the drawer a dry sprig that she held out to the flame.

But once again a flash of lightning pierced the windows and once again a thunderclap shook the house.

"Let's pray the Magnificat," said Joana.

"You pray, I don't know anything about it: those aren't things from my time," answered Gertrude.

And then through the beating down of the rain and the tumult of the storm there arose from the depths of the kitchen, Joana's voice, old, tired, and tremulous:

My soul doth magnify the Lord.
And my spirit hath rejoiced in God, my Savior.
For He hath regarded the low estate of his handmaiden: for
	behold from henceforth all generations shall call me blessed.
For he that is mighty hath done to me great things; and holy is
	his name.
And his mercy is on them that fear him from generation
	to generation.

Suddenly Joana grew silent.

"Are you finished?" asked Gertrude.

"No, I haven't finished; but I'm old, I've forgotten the rest of it."

However, from the other side of the kitchen, the voice of the man seated at the table of the poor rose up and carried on:

> He hath shewed strength with his arm; he hath scattered the
> proud in the imagination of their hearts.
> He hath put down the mighty from their seats, and exalted them
> of low degree.
> He hath filled the hungry with good things; and the rich he has
> sent empty away.

John, the son of the Lord of the Manor, was in the corridor when the lights went out. He had finished saying good night to everyone in the dining hall and was going to his room.

He stood alone in the darkness slashed by lightning. Pressed against the wall he could see a blue, unknown, and fantastic garden rise up outside from the darkness. Beauty, the abyss, and the clamor of the storm held him in suspense. He listened motionless for a time. Then he began to grow afraid. He felt himself alone in the midst of the storm. He wanted to run back to the hall, but he remembered the enormous shadow cast by the guest. Then his fear grew greater. He didn't dare go, in utter darkness, to meet the unknown guest. He pressed harder against the wall and cried out. At the end of the corridor, a light appeared.

It was the servant Antonio with the candles and the two maids. John ran to them and followed them.

The servants entered the pantry that was beside the dining room.

Antonio lit two big candlesticks and said:

"I can't remember a storm as bad as this one."

"And I can't remember a poor beggar wanting the Lord of the Manor to come and see him in the kitchen," said the chambermaid.

"What was that?" said John.

"There is a beggar who is in the kitchen and he wants them to call your father to talk to him."

"And why didn't they call him?"

"Because everything has its proper place and its proper time."

"What was he like?"

"He's like the other poor, he's like the folk from Varzim.

"Give me a candle," said John, "I want to go see him."

The servant gave him a candlestick with a candle and John went off with it.

When he opened the door of the kitchen, he saw, seated at the table of the poor, a man with a youthful and tired face. He was like the folk from Varzim, just as Julia the chambermaid had said. It seemed to John that he had known him for a long time.

Raising the candle, he walked toward the man and, when he was beside him, said slowly, in a low voice:

"Good evening."

"Good evening," answered the man.

There was a moment of silence. The storm seemed to have moved away and it had stopped raining.

"The storm is over," said the boy.

"It is over."

"Are you the man who asked them to call my father?"

"I am."

"Do you want to see my father?"

"I want your father to see me."

"What is your name?"

"Tell your father I have come on behalf of the Priest of Varzim."

Again, John looked at the man in silence. He lifted the candle a bit higher to see him more clearly. He said:

"I will get my father."

When John reached the top of the stairs the electric lights suddenly came on. The little boy blew out the candle, placed the candlestick on a table, and headed for the dining hall.

He entered and lifted his eyes: the shadow of the Important Man continued to creep along the walls and had occupied the entire ceiling. One could say that he was completely dominating that gathering of people.

And at a corner of the stove, enjoying the sweet warmth of the vine stump, the owner of the immense shadow was conversing with the Bishop and the Lord of the Manor.

"Father," said John, "there is a poor man in the kitchen who wants to talk to you."

"Not now. Tell him to come on Saturday."

"But it has to be today. It's very important."

"Why is it important?"

John didn't know what to say.

"Why not go see him?" The Bishop asked the Lord of the Manor. "A poor man always comes from God."

"The man down there," explained John, "says he has come from the Priest of Varzim."

The Lord of the Manor grew red. He stared hard at his son and said, pronouncing clearly and dryly every word:

"Tell him the Priest of Varzim knows I only receive the poor on Saturday. The man must come on Saturday."

"Father," John pleaded once again, "come to see him now."

"No," answered the Lord of the Manor.

John left the hall and returned to the kitchen.

For a moment he stared at the poor man in silence.

The rain had ceased. The only thing to be heard was the sound of Gertrude washing the pots and pans. Joana in her corner stared at the fire with an absent, faded gaze.

Finally John said:

"My father doesn't want to come. I asked him to, but he doesn't want to come."

"Thank you," said the man.

"When will I see you again?" asked John.

"Come see me in Varzim," the man answered.

Then he got up, said his good-byes, and left. John saw him disappear in the darkness, while from the open door there entered a green fragrance from the wet garden.

Gertrude approached the table of the poor to clear away the glass, the cutlery, and the plate.

"Look," she exclaimed, "the man didn't touch his food!"

"Ah!" said old Joana, lifting her head as if she had suddenly just awakened, "God also did not accept the offering of Cain."

"What tale is that?" asked the cook.

"It's a story from the beginning of the world," said the aged one. "It is the story of the children of Adam and Eve. They were called Cain and Abel. And Cain killed Abel, his brother."

III

Half an hour later, the Bishop was in his car, driving down the road. He was sad and bore a heavy heart. He was thinking of the Abbé of Varzim.

The Lord of the Manor and the Important Man had bewildered him with their good manners and their logical arguments. He was old. He no longer had the intelligence or the strength with which to struggle. He was tired of the world. His friends were his enemies; and his enemies were stronger than he. His thoughts were lost in darkness. He felt himself alone among men and God seemed to him infinitely obscured and veiled from sight. And the road that the headlights wrenched from the darkness, desolate between rows of naked trees, covered in mud, faded by winter, darkened by the night, seemed to him the very image of his soul.

The car left behind the curves of the mountains and entered a straight stretch.

In the distance, the headlights lit up a figure heading down the side of the road. The figure of a man walking by himself.

When the car passed by him, the Bishop said to the chauffeur: "Stop. Let's take him with us."

The Bishop rolled down the window and called out to the beggar:

"Where are you going?"

The man came closer and answered:

"I'm headed for the house of the Priest of Varzim."

"Oh! Are you coming from the Manor?"

"Yes, I am."

"Are you the man who asked to speak with the Lord of the Manor?"

"I am."

The Bishop looked at him. He was a man like many others. He reminded him of the people of Varzim. He had mud on his rags and hunger was written on his face. In his hands there was the gesture of patience. A very old gesture of patience. And all of a sudden it seemed to the old Bishop that he was gazing at all the abandonment of the world, all the suffering, all the loneliness, there in the face of that man. It was a hard thing to look at head-on.

For that reason, the Bishop averted his gaze while saying:

"Varzim is far away and the road is difficult. The ground has turned to mud and the downpour has filled the mountain paths with stones. Come with me and spend this night in my house."

The beggar did not answer.

The Bishop lifted his head, but all he saw before him was the night.

"Where are you, poor fellow?" he called.

But no one answered.

Then the old prelate got out of his car. He looked around and listened: on the road and in the fields he couldn't make out a single shape. He couldn't hear the slightest sound of footsteps. He told the chauffeur to look for the beggar. But the chauffeur couldn't find him either. The feet of the Bishop were now buried in the mud. The moon rose up through the clouds. But the moonlight only revealed an empty stretch of countryside, in which no one was moving away. The silence was attentive, suspended.

The Bishop covered his face with his hands. And then he tried to recognize within himself the man whom he had encountered. He remained like that for some time. Then he uncovered his face and murmured:

"What I have done must be undone."

Once again he got into the car and said to the chauffeur:

"We have to go back."

When they reached the Great House the lights were still on. But the sound of the horn at the gate at that time of night caused a great commotion.

A servant ran down the steps and came to open the gate. The key turned painfully in the lock and the iron gates creaked on their hinges. The Bishop's automobile entered, crossed the courtyard and came to a halt before the stone steps.

Curious to know what this visit in the middle of the night might be, the Lady of the Manor peeped through the curtains behind the window.

"The Bishop has come back!" she exclaimed in amazement.

And she went to let her husband know.

Hobbling slowly, the old Bishop climbed the staircase. He climbed with heavy steps, his back curved and his trembling hand supported on the balustrade of stone and moss. His shoes were covered in mud.

When he got to the top, the husband and wife were already awaiting him at the entrance.

The blue tiles glistened in the brightness of the night.

"I need to speak to you," said the Bishop to the Lord of the Manor.

"It is cold out here. It's better if we go inside."

In the hall the chairs seemed tense and afraid and the brightness of the late hour floated in the mirrors suddenly awakened by the light. The Bishop didn't want to take a seat and remained standing beside the table.

"No point in sitting down, I won't take long, what I have to say can be said quickly."

But he didn't know how to begin.

"Has something happened?" asked the Lord of the Manor.

"Yes, something has happened."

There was a new silence. Then, slowly, the Bishop said:

"I don't know how to tell you what I've seen. Today, this very night, a just man has been accused. But God himself came to testify on his behalf."

"I don't understand," said the Lord of the Manor.

"Today, here, the new Priest of Varzim was accused."

"And God came down from heaven to testify on his behalf?"

"That's right."

"I'm sorry, Reverend Bishop, I'm sorry but I cannot believe that."

The Bishop gazed at the Lord of the Manor, the master of the paintings, the silver plates, the fields, the vines, the pine groves, and the mountainsides. And he saw that it was as if all the things that that man owned had formed a thick wall around him, separating him from reality. He was enclosed in the certainty of his rights.

And, with sorrow, the Bishop answered:

"I know you cannot believe it."

Then, slowly, he went on:

"The Priest of Varzim was not only accused. He was also sold. Sold for the roof of a church. The Church of Our Lady of Hope."

The Lord of the Manor could hardly believe what he was hearing. For he had no intention of making a confession. It was as if he had lost or rejected long ago the possibility of recognizing his very self. Therefore he answered dryly, controlling his anger:

"I don't understand why you say sold. There was no sale. I gave an offering and I made, in accord with my conscience, a request."

"But I," confessed the Bishop with some bitterness, "promised to transfer the new priest to some other place. I made a promise and I accepted money. I cannot fulfill my promise and I wish to return the money to whoever gave it to me."

And the wrinkled hand placed two checks upon the table.

The Lord of the Manor gazed at the gesture with a mixture of rage, shock, and indignation. The Bishop, that polished prelate, was betraying the rules of the game. To the rules of good manners he was responding with problems of conscience. He was accusing him, the Lord of the Manor, of engaging in unconfessable and confused dealings. He was accusing him in clear words, unmistakably. He wasn't even expressing himself indirectly or through allusions. And, in the depth of his soul, the Lord of the Manor had a strong desire to take back the money and to give the Bishop a crude response. But he remembered that it would be unseemly to have contentions with the Bishop, he remembered his fame, his reputation, and the good manners he had been taught when little. Therefore he controlled himself and said with some pomp:

"I don't understand. The money I gave has nothing to do with the Priest of Varzim. They are two completely different issues. Your Exalted Reverence is making a lamentable mistake. I gave an offering and I will never accept back what I gave. But this question cannot be resolved by just the two of us. We have to find out what my guest thinks about it."

The Lord of the Manor rang for a servant and sent him to call for the Important Man.

But the servant Antonio searched the house in vain. The Important Man, the unexpected overnight guest, had disappeared. He was neither in his room nor in any of the halls, nor on the stairs, nor in the corridors. His car and his chauffeur had evaporated into thin air, and even the tire marks of his car in the wet gravel of the courtyard had disappeared.

This news troubled the Lord of the Manor. He left his wife in the sitting room as company to the Bishop and went himself, ahead of the servants, to make a thorough examination of the house and gardens. They climbed up to the attic, they went down to the cellar, they peeked into the well. Antonio looked behind the curtains; Mariana, the chambermaid, looked under the bed. The Lord of the Manor looked behind the shrubs. But the man who had disappeared did not appear.

The search over, the Bishop, the Lord and Lady of the Manor, the servant Antonio, Julia, the serving maid, and Mariana, the chambermaid, united in their astonishment, stood around in a circle in the sitting room, discussing what had happened. The Lord of the Manor begged the Bishop to forgive him for the strangeness of the situation. There was no possible explanation. There hovered in the air a heavy sense of unease. The Lady of the Manor shivered when the wooden floorboards creaked and, outside, the shadows in the garden had begun to look suspicious.

Finally, the Bishop spoke:

"It is late. Tomorrow we will be able to think more clearly. Your guest will certainly appear or send some sort of message. I will now leave. I will leave with you the two checks."

But when they looked down at the table they could see only one check. It belonged to the Lord of the Manor. The other, the check from the Important Man, had disappeared.

Everyone looked at each other in consternation. Hands and eyes traveled nervously all over the room in search of the little piece of paper.

"Look under the table," said the Lady of the Manor to the servant.

Antonio got down on his hands and knees and dove beneath the red silk tablecloth. After a few moments, with the gesture of an old-time photographer re-emerging with his head from the drapes of his apparatus, he reappeared and said:

"It isn't there."

"Was it written out to cash or in your name?" the Lord of the Manor asked the Bishop.

"I don't know, I didn't look," admitted the Bishop, perturbed.

The confusion grew.

"We have to let the bank know," said the Lord of the Manor. "Your Supreme Reverence noticed the name of the bank?"

"No, I didn't notice."

Complications were growing.

But the Bishop had now grown tired of the business of this world.

"I will leave the affair in your hands," he said to the Lord of the Manor. "The night will bring some guidance. And tomorrow, the day will bring some clarification. I will now be going."

He turned to say good-bye and then he left.

After the Bishop's departure, the Lord of the Manor set the servants to looking for the check. They looked beneath the carpets, the cushions on the sofa, the magazines that were on top of the table. But after half an hour, the check still had not appeared.

Finally, the master said to the servants:

"I'm going to bed. Continue your search; the check cannot have disappeared. Good night."

He left, and Antonio, Julia, and Mariana looked at one another dejectedly.

"You two stay here and look, I'll look for it in the hallways. Maybe the check flew off with a draft," said the servant Antonio.

"Or maybe the Devil carried it off," said the serving maid Julia.

Antonio searched the floor in all the corridors without much hope and then went to the kitchen to unburden himself to Gertrude.

"But, in the end," asked the cook, "who was that gentleman who was so important?"

"I don't know," answered the servant, "I only know that it feels as if the Devil had entered the house."

"Who knows!" said old Joana, gazing with her tired eyes at the fire. "Who knows! Maybe he really was the Devil! These days it could easily be true."

"These days," said the cook, "there is no longer any God or any Devil. There are just the rich and the poor. And each man for himself."

And, grabbing a rag, Gertrude cleaned up the footprints left on the floor by the beggar.

two

— ❧ —

THE JOURNEY

The road passed through fields, and sometimes, in the distance, one could make out mountains. It was early September and the morning stretched across the earth, filled with light and plenitude. Everything seemed aglow.

And inside the car carrying them forward, the woman said to the man:

"This is the middle of our life."

Outside the windows, things were rushing by. Houses, bridges, mountains, villages, trees, and rivers were in flight and seemed one after another to have been devoured. As if the road itself were swallowing them up.

They came to a crossing. There they turned to the right. And they went on.

"We must be getting there," said the man.

And they continued on their way.

Trees, fields, houses, bridges, mountains, rivers, rushed by, slipping into the distance.

The woman looked nervously about and said:

"We must have made a mistake. We must have taken the wrong road."

"It must have happened at the crossroads," said the man, stopping the car. "We turned to the west, we should have turned to the east. Now we have to go back to the crossroads."

The woman leaned her head back and saw how high the sun had risen in the sky and how things were slowly losing their shadows. She also noticed that the dew on the grass along the roadside had already dried.

"Let's go," she said.

The man turned the wheel, the car made a U-turn, and they headed back down the road.

The woman, tired, closed her eyes for a bit, leaned her head against the back of the seat and began to imagine the place to which they were going. It was a place to which they had never gone before. They didn't even know anyone who had ever been there. They only knew of it from the map and by name. It was said to be a wonderful place.

She imagined that the house would be calm and silent, filled with peace and whiteness, surrounded by rosebushes, and she imagined that the garden would be large and green, traversed by murmurings.

And someone had told her that through the garden there passed a glistening, crystal-clear river. And that one could see sand and clean polished pebbles at the bottom of the river. And along the banks grew fine grass, mixed with clover. And trees with rounded canopies, laden with fruit, grew in those meadows.

"As soon as we get there," she said, "we'll take a swim in the river."

"We'll take a swim in the river and then we'll lie down and rest in the grass," said the man, his eyes always on the road.

And she imagined with thirst the clear, cold water around her shoulders, and she imagined the grass where they would lie down side by side, beneath the shade of leafy, fruit-laden trees. There they would stay. There, there would be time to rest one's eyes on things.

There, there would be time to touch things. There one would be able to slowly breathe in the fragrance of the rosebushes. There, all would be slowness and presence. There, there would be silence in which to listen to the clear murmur of the river. Silence in which to say grave pure words laden with peace and joy. There nothing would be lacking: being there would be the one desire.

Outside the windows, fields, pine groves, hills, and rivers were rushing by.

"We should be getting to the crossroads," the man said.

And they went on.

Rivers, fields, pine groves, and hills. Another half hour passed.

"We should have reached the crossroads by now," said the man.

"We must have taken a wrong turn somewhere," said the woman.

"No, we couldn't have made a mistake," said the man, "there was no other road."

And they went on.

"The crossroads should have appeared by now," said the man.

"What are we going to do?" asked the woman.

"Keep on going."

"But we are getting lost."

"I don't see any other road," said the man.

And they went on.

They encountered rivers, fields, hillsides; they crossed rivers, passed through fields and hillsides; they left rivers, fields, hillsides behind. The countryside rushed by, sucked away.

"We're getting more and more lost," said the woman.

"But is there another road?" asked the man.

And he stopped the car.

On the left there was a large stretch of empty grassland; to the right a hill covered with trees.

"Let's go to the top of the hill," said the man. "From there we should be able to see all the roads around."

They climbed to the top of the hill, but they could not see any roads at all; however, they did see a man digging in a garden.

They walked toward him and they asked him if he knew the way to the crossroads.

"Yes," said the man with the hoe, "it's that way."

"Could you show us the way?"

"Yes, I can, but first I have to finish this ditch to water the vegetables. It won't take long."

"We'll wait," said the man.

"I'm thirsty," said the woman.

"Over there, beyond the boulders," said the man with the hoe, gesturing, "there's a spring. Go there for a drink while I finish digging this ditch."

They went in the direction the man with the hoe had pointed and behind the boulders they found the spring.

The spring water fell from high above and plunged straight down into the earth, crystal clear and glistening like a sword.

There they drank and their faces and hair got splattered with water, and they laughed with joy in the freshness of the water, forgetting their fatigue, the journey, the lost way. The woman sat down on a rock covered with moss, the man sat down beside her, and the two remained there for a while, hand in hand, motionless and silent.

Then a bird settled close to the spring and the man said:

"We have to go."

They got up and headed back to the garden, to look for the man with the hoe.

But when they got to the garden, the man with the hoe wasn't there. They saw the water flowing through the irrigation ditch; they saw the parsley and mint growing side by side; but they did not see the man with the hoe.

"He didn't want to wait," said the man.

"Why did he lie to us?"

"Maybe he didn't intend to lie. Maybe he just couldn't wait. Or maybe he forgot about us."

"Now what?" asked the woman.

"Let's go back to the car and let's go in the direction he was pointing."

They went up the hill and back down in the direction of the car, but when they got to the road the car had disappeared.

"We must have gone wrong; we must have gone in a different direction."

"Or someone stole our car."

"Where could the man with the hoe have gone?"

"Maybe he went to the spring looking for us."

"We have to find someone," said the woman.

"Let's go back to the spring; I'm sure the man with the hoe went there."

And they headed back again.

They went up the hill and back down again; they crossed the vegetable garden.

They could smell the mint and the watered earth. But on the other side of the boulders they did not find the spring.

"It wasn't here," said the man.

"It was here," said the woman. "It was here. I'm scared. Let's go right back to the road."

And they went back to the road to look for the car.

"What'll we do?" asked the woman.

"Someone will be passing by," said the man.

They followed the road. The sun continued to climb in the sky. "I'm tired," said the woman.

"When we get to the place we're going, you can rest, stretched out on the grass, in the shade of the trees with their fruit."

"We really have to find the road," said the woman.

In the distance, among the pines, appeared a house.

"Let's go there," said the man. "Maybe there is someone there who can tell us the right way to go."

There was a light breeze and the pines were swaying.

They knocked on the door of the house. No one answered. They listened and they seemed to hear voices. They knocked again. No one answered. They waited. Once again they knocked, loudly, deliberately, clearly, slowly. The blows echoed. No one answered.

Then the man lowered his right shoulder and forced open the door. The house was empty.

It was a small, simple house for country folk. A bare house, where the gestures of life alone had been written. There was a kitchen and two bedrooms. On a mantel on the whitewashed wall stood an image: in front of the image an oil lamp was burning; to the side, someone had placed a bouquet of blessed Easter flowers.

There was no one in the kitchen. There was no one in the bedrooms. There was no one out back, where laundry was drying, hanging from the line, gesticulating in the breeze.

In the oven the ashes were still warm and atop the table there was wine and bread.

"I'm hungry," said the woman.

They sat down and ate.

"What now?" said the woman.

"Let's go back to the road again and keep on going," said the man.

They went out and passed through the pine grove. But the road had disappeared.

"I'm scared," said the woman. "I'm getting more and more scared. Everything is disappearing."

"We're together," said the man.

"But what can we do without a road?"

"Let's go back to the house," said the man, "and wait there until the owners come home and show us the way and help us out."

And once again they crossed through the pines. But in the spot where the house had been now there was just a small clearing and stones scattered about.

They both fell silent. Then the woman crumbled to the ground and, stretched out among the stones, cried and cried with her face pressed to the earth.

"Let's go," said the man.

"Where to?" she asked.

"We have to find some kind of road."

"Why should we? We lose everything that we find."

The man knelt down beside the woman and cleaned her face of tears and earth.

Then he helped her up and the two of them went onward.

They crossed through the pines and they found a field.

But they didn't see any road at all.

In the middle of the field stood an apple tree filled with red apples, polished and round.

"They're beautiful," said the woman.

She picked one for herself and another for the man. The two of them sat down on the fine grass, beneath the comforting shade of the tree, and the firm, fresh, and clean flesh of the apples snapped between their teeth.

It was already early afternoon and, in the luminous day, leaning against the hard, dark, rough trunk, they rested in silence, hearing nothing but the gentle murmur of the earth beneath the sun.

Then the man said:

"Let's go."

They got up and they went on.

When they were already at the end of the field, next to the hedge that separated it from the next field, the woman exclaimed:

"We should have picked a few apples to bring along with us. We don't know where we are, or how far we still have to go before we find something else to eat again."

"That's true," said the man.

And, going back, they walked toward the apple tree standing out so roundly in the middle of the field.

However, when they got to the tree, they saw that on the branches, among the leaves, all the fruit had disappeared.

"Someone must have passed by without our noticing and picked all the apples," said the man.

"Oh!" said the woman, "so quickly! Everything is disappearing so quickly! We find things. They are there. But when we come back they have already disappeared. And we don't even know who has erased them or carried them away."

With heads lowered they returned to their path.

They crossed field after field, but they never found anyone who could answer their questions and give them advice. Next to a hedge they saw a cork tankard and an earthenware pitcher on the ground.

The woman opened the tankard and looked inside the pitcher.

"They're empty," she said.

"Where's the owner?"

They looked around but they didn't see anyone. They called, but no one answered.

"Maybe he's on the other side of the hedge," said the woman.

They crossed through the hedge, but on the other side they didn't see anyone at all. All they saw was a small rill flowing almost hidden among the clover and the watercress. Kneeling down, they washed their hands and their faces. From the hollow of her hands the woman drank and gave drink to the man.

"If we had brought the pitcher," she said, "we could have taken some water along with us."

"And in the cork tankard, we could have carried some fruit. Let's go back and look for the tankard and the pitcher."

They crossed back through the hedge.

But the pitcher was broken and the cork container was completely eaten away.

"Who could have broken it?"

"Maybe the wind or some animal passing by."

"Who could have gnawed up the cork?"

"Mice, snakes, moles, stray dogs."

"Broken and gnawed away, they're no longer any good."

"Let's get out of here," said the woman.

It was already midafternoon when they came upon a vast forest, from whose edge a path emerged.

"Let's take the path. Wherever it goes, we'll have to find people. Paths are made for people to go on. Paths are made to go to places where there are people."

And they entered the forest.

Oaks, chestnuts, lindens, birches, cedars, and pines crossed their branches. Broad rays of sunlight slanted between the trunks. The air was green and golden.

"What a lovely forest!" exclaimed the woman.

"What a lovely forest!" exclaimed the man.

Here and there a dry branch snapped. Now and then a pine cone would drop from above. One could hear the murmur of the breeze high among the leaves. One could hear the song of hidden birds. One could hear the silence of the moss and of the earth.

And lulled by the beauty, the music, and the fragrance of the forest, the man and the woman went on hand in hand down the path.

Until they heard in the distance the sound of chopping.

They kept on walking and they came closer to the sound.

"It's coming from there!" said the woman.

And leaving the path they headed to the right.

They found a woodsman splitting wood.

"We're lost," said the man, "we're looking for a way back to the main road."

"Just keep to the path," said the woodsman, "and you'll come to the main road."

"Thank you," said the man.

And the two of them turned back.

But they couldn't find the path.

"How could we have lost it?" asked the woman.

"Let's ask the woodsman to guide us," said the man.

They went back to the spot where they had spoken with the woodsman. But all they found was split wood. The woodsman had disappeared.

"He's gone," said the woman.

"He can't be far off. Let's call to him."

They called again and again. But no voice, no human sound, answered them. All they heard were the songs of the birds, the sounds of dry branches cracking, the murmur of the breeze in the leaves.

"Let's listen silently," said the man. "He can't be far away yet, maybe we can still hear the sound of his footsteps."

And they listened in silence.

But all they heard were the sounds of the forest.

"I know a better way to listen," said the woman.

And she got down on her knees and placed first one ear, then the other, to the ground.

But all she heard was the pulsing silence of the earth.

"All I hear is the earth," she said.

"Let's go on," answered the man.

And they went on.

They found a hedge heavy with mulberries.

"They're wonderful!" said the woman.

The man picked a handful of mulberries and held them out on his palm to the woman. She tried them and said again:

"They're wonderful!"

Laughing, the two of them began to pick mulberries and, having gathered together a large amount, they sat down on the ground and began to eat them. The slanting light of afternoon passed between the dark trunks and lit the green of the grasses. When they had finished eating, the man said:

"We have to go. We have to find the main road and the place where we are going."

"How are we going to find that place if we don't even know where we are?"

"We have to try," answered the man.

They got up to leave.

"Wait," said the woman. "I want to bring along some berries."

And, untying the knot of the kerchief round her neck, she opened it and spread it wide upon the ground. The two of them began to pick berries and they piled up a large pyramid on the kerchief. Then they tied together, two by two, the four corners of the kerchief.

"Let's go," said the man, passing his finger through the two knots.

And they went again along their way.

They went along hand in hand through the green and golden air.

"This forest is beautiful!" said the woman.

"It is," said the man, "but we still haven't found the main road."

The woman, however, bent her head back and breathed in deeply the smell of the trees and the earth. She stretched her hand out into the air and a butterfly settled on her fingertips.

"Ah!" she said, "even lost, look how everything is fragrant and lovely. Even not knowing if we will ever arrive, I feel like laughing and singing in honor of the things around us. Even on this road that leads I don't know where, the trees are green and fresh as if nourished by a deep certainty. Even here the light settles gently on our faces as if it recognizes us. I am filled with fear and I am filled with joy."

"The air and the light," said the man, "are good and beautiful. If we were not lost, this walk would be a wonderful journey. But the air and the light don't know how to tell us the way."

They could hear a small crystalline murmuring and, after a few more steps, they came to a river.

It was a little river, narrow and clear, and along its banks grew pink and white wildflowers.

The man and the woman lay face down on the ground and, bending toward the water, began to drink.

"How clear the water is!" exclaimed the woman. "Let's go for a swim."

The got undressed and they entered the river.

Now laughing, now in silence, they swam for a long time. They dove down with eyes open, touching the little polished pebbles at the bottom, passing through a world in suspension, transparent and green. Blue trout glided by close to their gestures.

Afterward, they stretched out on the grassy banks in the golden shade of the forest. The profile of the woman stood sharply outlined among the flowers.

"This is almost like the place we're going to," she said.

"It is," the man answered, "but this is just a stop along the way."

And they both got up and got dressed.

"Shall we go?" he asked.

"Wait a minute," the woman answered. "First I want to pick some flowers to take along."

She knelt on the ground and began to make a bouquet. And the man noticed that she was pulling the flowers up by their roots and he asked:

"Why are you pulling the flowers up by their roots?"

"Because I want to plant them in the place to which we're going. I don't know if they have flowers like these there," answered the woman.

And they went on.

Now day was waning.

"I'm hungry," said the woman.

"We have the mulberries," said the man.

They placed the kerchief on the ground and untied the knots.

But the kerchief was empty.

For a while they said nothing. Then the man said:

"It must be that we didn't tie the knots of the corners well, and the berries fell out one by one as we were walking. One by one. I didn't even notice as they fell."

"I'm hungry," said the woman.

"Let's go on," said the man.

They could see far off between the trees a red glow.

"It's the sunset!" exclaimed the woman. "The sun is already setting!"

"Let's get going," said the man. "Night is falling and we still haven't found the road."

And they went off, almost running.

Among the shadows of dusk they suddenly heard voices.

"People!" exclaimed the man. "We're saved!"

"Saved?" wondered the woman.

And again they heard voices.

"They're off that way," said the woman, pointing to the left.

"No, they're over there," said the man, pointing to the right.

The man grabbed the woman's hand and the two went running off to the right.

But the more they ran, the more distant the voices sounded.

"They're going faster than we are!" the woman complained.

"But," said the man, "if we can at least manage to follow the way they're going, we'll be saved."

And so they went, listening and running, while the shadows of dusk continued to grow. Until finally the voices could no longer be heard and night closed round them, thick and heavy.

The moon had not yet risen. On all sides they were surrounded by shadows, noises, rustlings they mistook for shapes, steps, voices. But they were just dark shadows, the trunks of trees, dry branches crackling, the murmuring of the leaves.

"Are we lost?" the woman asked.

"We don't know," said the man.

Slowly they went on, hand in hand, in silence, leaning on each other.

Until suddenly they saw that they had come to the end of the forest.

Filled with hope, they hurried toward the open space but, leaving the trees behind, they found before them an abyss.

Leaning over, they looked down. However, by the light of the stars, they couldn't see anything in front of them except a pool of darkness, while the coldness of marble touched their face.

"It's a cliff," said the man. "The land is broken before us. We can't go on, not one more step."

"Look!" said the woman.

And she pointed to a narrow path that clung to the edge of

the abyss. To the left was a high wall of stone and to the right the void.

"Let's go," said the man.

"I'm afraid," said the woman.

"We're together," answered the man, "don't be afraid."

And they continued on the path.

The man went ahead and the woman behind held to the rocks with her left hand and with her right the man's shoulder.

They went on in silence beneath the dark gleam of the stars, measuring each gesture and each step.

But suddenly the body of the man wavered, and little stones went rolling. He cried out to the woman:

"Hold me!"

But already his shoulder was slipping from her hands. And the woman screamed:

"Grab hold of the earth!"

But no voice answered her, for in the great, clear-cut sonorous silence only the rolling of stones could be heard.

She was alone, wrapped in terror, clinging to the ground, facing the void.

"Hello!" she screamed, bending over the abyss.

Far off, the echo of her voice repeated:

"Hello!"

She was stretched along the ground, her hands buried in the earth, and she began to scream like someone lost in the middle of a dream. Then she stopped screaming and murmured:

"I have to go and look for him."

She went on, crawling along the path, touching the ground with her hands as she searched for a passage through which she could go down to look for the man. But there was no passage.

Then she tried going down the very slope of the abyss itself.

Clinging to grasses and roots she let herself slide down the prec-
ipice. But her feet found no support to stand on. For the face
dropped straight down: it was a smooth wall of naked rock.

"I have to go back to the path," thought the woman, "and look
for a way through further along."

And, clinging to grasses and roots, she dragged herself up to
the path.

But the path had disappeared. Now there was just a narrow
ledge where she couldn't fit, where not even her feet could fit. A
ledge with no way out. There she remained, sideways, one foot in
front of the other, the right side of her body pressed to the stone
face and her left side already bathed by the cold and hoarse breath
of the abyss. She could feel that the grasses and roots she was
holding on to were slowly giving way with the weight of her body.
She understood that now it was she who would fall into the abyss.
She saw that, when the roots snapped, she would have nothing to
cling to, not even herself. For it was her very self that she was now
about to lose.

She understood that only a few moments remained to her.

Then she turned her face toward the far side of the abyss. She
tried to gaze through the darkness. But only darkness could be
seen. Even so, she thought:

"Surely there is someone on the other side of the abyss."

And she began to call.

three

—❧—

PORTRAIT OF

MONICA

Monica is such an extraordinary person that she manages to be a good housewife and super chic, to be director of the International League of Useless Women, to help her husband with the business, to do her gymnastics every morning, be punctual, have an enormous number of friends, give lots of dinners, go to lots of dinners, not smoke, not grow older, to like everyone, be liked by everyone, speak well of everyone, be well spoken of by everyone, collect seventeenth-century spoons, play golf, go to bed late, get up early, eat yogurt, do yoga, like abstract art, be a member of all the musical societies, always be amused, be a fine example of the virtues, be very successful and very serious—all at the same time.

I have known many people similar to Monica in my life. But, in reality, they are mere parodies of her. They always forget either the yoga or the abstract art.

Behind all this lies hard work without respite and a rigorous, constant discipline. One could say that Monica works from dawn to dusk.

As a matter of fact, in order to gain all that success and all those glorious possessions, Monica has had to renounce three things: poetry, love, and holiness.

Poetry is offered to each person just once and the effect of refusal is irreversible. Love is offered rarely and those who refuse it a few times never find it again. But holiness is offered anew to everyone each day, and therefore those who renounce holiness are obliged to repeat their refusal every day.

This forces Monica to maintain severe discipline. As they say in the circus, "any distraction could cause the death of the artist." Monica is never distracted. All her dresses are well chosen and all her friends are useful. Like a precise instrument, she measures the degree of utility of each situation and every person. And like a well-trained horse, she does her jumps without touching a thing and always has a clean round. For this reason everything goes well for her, even her sufferings.

Monica's dinners also always go well. Each setting is an investment. The food is excellent and, as for conversation, everyone is always in agreement, since Monica never invites people who might have inconvenient opinions. She places her intelligence at the service of stupidity. Or, more precisely: her intelligence springs from the stupidity of others. This is the form of intelligence that guarantees control. And that is why Monica's kingdom is solid and large.

She is intimate with mandarins and bankers and also with manicurists, clerks, and hairdressers. When she arrives at the hairdresser or at a shop, she always speaks in a louder tone of voice, so everyone will realize that she has arrived. And manicurists and clerks throw themselves at her. Monica's arrival is always, everywhere, a success. When she is at the beach, the sun itself grows somewhat dim.

Monica's husband is a poor drip whom Monica has transformed into a most important man. From this tedious husband, Monica has drawn the maximum return. She helps him, advises him, rules him. When he is named chief executive of yet another thing, it is Monica who is really chosen. They are not man and woman. They are not their marriage. They are, rather, two partners working for the triumph of the same firm. The contract that unites them is indissoluble, for divorce is the ruin of the social set. The world of business is most correct.

And that is why Monica, having renounced holiness, dedicates herself with great energy to works of charity. She knits sweaters for the children that her friends condemn to hunger. Occasionally, by the time the scarves are done, the children have already starved to death. But life goes on. And Monica's success as well. Each year she appears younger. Poverty, humiliation, ruin don't even graze the hem of her dress. Between her and the lowly, the downtrodden, there is nothing in common.

And for this reason Monica has the best of relations with the Prince of this World. She is his faithful backer, singer of his virtues, admirer of his silences and speeches. Admirer of his work, which is at her service; admirer of his spirit, which she serves.

One could say that in every building constructed in these times there has always been a stone provided by Monica.

I haven't seen Monica now in several months. Recently I heard that, at a certain party, she spent a good deal of time in conversation with the Prince of this World. The two of them spoke with great intimacy. Of course, there's nothing wrong with that. Everyone knows that Monica is as serious as they come and everyone knows that the Prince of this World is an austere and chaste man.

It isn't the desire of love that unites them. What unites them, in fact, is a will devoid of love.

And it's only natural that he should show his gratitude to Monica in public. Everyone knows that she is his greatest supporter, the firm foundation of all his power.

four

— ❧ —

BEACH

It was a kind of summer club, a great square house painted yellow
and a veranda filled with vast greenness that opened on an avenue
where magnificent plane trees inhabited the night.

It smelled of the sea and of fruit. Lengthy harmonies seemed
suspended from the trees and the stars. And among the white
houses, in the dark blue night, passed the rolling of the sea.

All this surrounded the club and its walls and windows, its doors
and chairs. And even more, it surrounded, intensely, one by one,
each person there.

One entered the hall through a large door that was always open.

The hall was enormous and in the middle there was a nostalgic
palm tree. The decorations were from 1920, in a special style that
only existed in that region.

On green benches, lining the white walls, covered half way up
by green trellis-work, there were small groups of people seated
before green tables.

There were three dark groups of men and two lighter groups of
women of a certain age.

As I crossed the great hall, I said "good evening" to the various
groups. Then I took a look through the game-room door, which
was made of glass. The card players seemed like condemned men
trying to amuse themselves calmly during their last hours. They

were abstracted, in abeyance, and didn't notice me. I went back across the hall and entered the ballroom.

It was orchestra day. The orchestra came twice a week from a nearby beach resort. The musicians were thin and young and wore old smoking jackets, slightly tarnished from use and from the humidity of maritime winters. They were failed musicians: with little artistry, little money, and no fame. They must have been either resigned or seething. I hope they were seething: that would have been less sad. A man in revolt, even if inglorious, is never completely defeated. But passive resignation, resignation through a progressive deafening of one's being, that is a complete failure and without cure. But those in revolt, even those for whom everything—lamplight and the light of spring—hurts like a knife, those who cut themselves on the air and in their very gestures, are the honor of the human condition. They are the ones who do not accept imperfection. And therefore their souls are like a vast desert without shade or freshness where the fire burns without being consumed.

And so there we were laughing, conversing, dancing, while the musicians, in their old smoking jackets, played on.

Sometimes someone would complain that they were playing badly.

Through the open windows the music would float out and lose itself among the foliage of the plane trees, mixing with the slight tremor of the breeze and the deep reverberation of the sea.

The ballroom was long and wide. There were two doors leading to the veranda, two doors leading to the entrance hall, and a fifth door that led to a smaller hall which served as a passage and connection between the ballroom and the bar.

At the back of the ballroom there was a stage where the musicians would play, but on which no dramatic event was ever enacted. But it was known that in the past there had been theatrical presentations.

Along the wall to the left of the stage there were three windows that opened onto a quiet little street where hardly anyone ever went by.

Sometimes in between dances we would come and lean out at the windows: across the way was a house with white walls, where the moonlight turned blue and where the shadows of leaves filled with gestures appeared, quivering, restless, and alive.

And we would stretch out an arm and pull from the branches a leaf, which we would slowly crunch between our teeth.

Then we would breathe in the aroma of the linden trees and lift our heads to the sky filled with stars and say:

"What a beautiful night!"

At other times, when we didn't dance, we would talk in small groups, seated on the long sofas covered in green that lined the walls. There would be the light murmur of adolescent loves. It was like the murmur of the breeze. For it was the beginning of life and so far nothing had happened to us. So far, nothing was grave, tragic, naked and bloody.

And the night outside, with its mixed aromas, with its murmurs and its silences and its shadows and lights, seemed the face of a promise.

But I don't think that anyone there at that time really thought about the future. Only perhaps two or three, whose lives, later on, so efficient and well organized, always had the air of something previously arranged. But only those. All the others made no plans about the future. For them, the present was a limitless expanse of the available, of suspense and of choice. They didn't plan the future—merely, in a vague way, they awaited it.

And so vaguely that often it was as if they were awaiting not the future, but the past.

For there one talked a great deal about the past. Constantly in those conversations stories were told of earlier generations, stories of a time when existence was more defined and visible, a time when feelings turned to actions and destinies were utterly fulfilled.

Sometimes, all of a sudden, deep inside a mirror, there would be a splendor that was the splendor of some ancient time. And then it was as if the ancient nights of August and the long-gone September afternoons could, like Dom Sebastião, come again.

On the avenues, among the linden trees, on the verandas, in the sound of footsteps along the streets of sand and gravel, turning over loose stones, in the sea, like a seashell repeating the roar of a tempestuous past, and even in the floor, the tables, and the chairs, there seemed to be suspended the hope of a return.

And as the night deepened and almost everyone would leave, as it grew later and later, the expectation would become almost conscious, almost visible. One might have said that lost time was rising up and turning tangible.

People would drift off, the halls would grow empty, and a question and a silence would hover in the air, as if something, something obscurely desired and promised, had not occurred.

The musicians would put away their instruments and close the piano. Dark and thin, they would come down the steps from the stage and then disappear, I suppose through a trapdoor, for I never saw them leave by any ordinary door. Or perhaps they just dissolved into thin air. Or perhaps they were gods from Persia and had come during the night on a magic carpet in order to contemplate, disguised as musicians, the end of Western sensibility.

For the expectation, the expectation of fantastic things, visible and real, the expectation of things destined, promised, sensed, was growing almost lucidly hallucinatory.

Leaning against the doorpost, a lone man, tall and thin like a tree in winter, took out his pocket watch and checked the time. Then he quickly put the watch away, as if he were ashamed of time.

We were all waiting.

Already there were not many of us and the ballroom lights went out; the great hall was deserted, in the game room there were only four card players still waiting for death, and when we entered the bar a man, the same one as always, turned round on his high barstool and, bringing his glass with him, came to sit with us at a table.

And it was hard to say from what era he came; for he clearly had the voice, the gaze, the gestures of a figure from stories of olden times. But not the destiny, not the lived life. It was as if he had rejected all destiny, all lived life, as if it were something alien, exterior and false, and for him that moment, that bar, that table, that conversation, that glass were enough.

It was as if he had wanted to keep his being totally separate from lived life, since in life there was no act in which being could be realized and concrete existence was just debasement, falsification, profanation.

And so he had decided to use his own life as if it didn't belong to him, to use it the way the musicians of the orchestra used their rented evening jackets.

The late hour was diffusing, multiplying, and isolating everything.

Almost everyone was gone, and emptiness was settling gently on the tables and chairs, while the night, with the vast shadows of its trees mingling with the sound of the sea, drifted in through the open window.

And the man who had come to sit with us spoke on, mixing his words with time, the night, the tumult of the sea, the breath of the breeze among the leaves. And from his words a great image grew forth, blossoming out and spreading toward countless spaces.

His sensibility was so perfect that even on the very wood of the table his hand reposed with tenderness. As he spoke, his eyes widened, blue with the blue of an alcohol flame. And his gaze grew boundless and impersonal as if he were seeing something else beyond us. Perhaps:

> The distant memory of a land
> Eternal but long lost and we not knowing
> If we've lost it in the past or in the future.

And, as he went on talking, the image born from his words would take shape within the souls of those listening to him, like a myth. He was like a limit, like a boundary marker that said:

"From this point on the sea is no longer navigable."

And yet, he could not be mistaken for a god. Among the gods, to be and to exist are united. In him, lived life wasn't even the servant of being, wasn't even the ground on which being set foot, but was mere chance without nexus, a failed meeting, an accident without form and without truth, a disdained accident.

I was seated opposite him, on the other side of the small table. For a long time he remained silent. Then he leaned over the table and said:

"Listen."

> There is a sea,
> A far and distant sea
> Beyond the farthest line,
> Where all my ships that went astray,
> Where all my dreams of yesterday
> Are mine.

Outside the streetlights had long ago been extinguished.

It was late. And the gleam of the late hour gently glided over the hands and the glasses on the polished tabletop.

The moon had already disappeared and a mist, airy and white, was beginning to rise from the sea and come through the open window.

"The mist has come back," someone said.

We looked out the window. The fragrance coming now from outside was fresher and smelled more of the sea.

Now and then far off one could hear the whistling of trains. They were the endless freight trains with early-morning goods, their cars laden with salt, cattle, wood, and stones. And the signal woman, standing tall, held up a green lantern at the end of her extended arm. And a long trail of melancholy seemed to settle and then slowly dissolve over the lands through which the train was passing.

It was late.

A waiter, half asleep, was wandering among the tables.

"Look at this," said one of my friends, pointing to some pages in an opened illustrated magazine.

Cities and more cities bombed out, ships, cannons, planes, war machines, the ridiculous Führer, captain of stupidity, bestiality, and disaster, leading his people.

And suddenly a violent, rapid-fire discussion arose. But, despite the discussion and the photographs, the war seemed unreal and abstract, as if we were talking about the invasion of the barbarians or the torments of the year 2000. The war was far away.

Then the man with the pocket watch arose and said:

"I'm going to listen to the news."

Behind him the door swung to and fro.

A few moments later one could hear from the nearby hall the

sound of the wireless mixed with scraps of music and foreign tongues.

Then a voice began to speak clearly.

I got up and went to listen.

Rommel is retreating in the desert, the news was saying.

And suddenly, for me, through the power of a name, the war became real.

I went back to the bar and sat down again at the same table, in the midst of all the talk.

Rommel was retreating in the desert.

And I tried to imagine the blue night of the desert where the silent men were retreating. I tried to imagine the shadows and the sweetness of the sand, the clear brilliance of the stars, the mystery, the tensely felt presence of an invisible enemy, the edge of death, the terror, the passion and the dense, sharp, and exact weight of each moment. And I tried to imagine the men. The men: οἳ ανθρωποι. The men: clearly defeated, fighting in retreat, surrounded by death, measuring out their gestures, measuring the measure of the efficacy of their gestures, battling each foot of the way, knowing their cause unjust, their battle lost. Clearly defeated, battling beneath the clear brilliance of the stars.

And it was late.

So late that we all got up and left, while, half asleep, the waiter took from our table all our glasses which, bumping against each other, continued to clink and tinkle on his tray.

Outside, no sooner had we passed through the door leading onto the veranda, than a vast breath from the sea covered us, surrounded us, invaded us.

The mist from the sea had transfigured everything.

Now there was only the smell of the sea. The passionate aroma of seaweed dripped from the trees. Moon and stars could not be seen.

Not even the plane trees could be seen. All one could see were white walls in the white mist. Everything was motionless and in suspense.

All one could hear was the voice of the sea, astonishingly real, endlessly remaking itself.

And it seemed as if the vast, violent green depth of the sea, as if it were our natural destiny, was calling us.

five

HOMER

When I was little, a wandering, crazed old man we called Buzio, or Seashell, would sometimes pass by on the beach.

Buzio was like a Manueline monument: everything about him reminded one of the sea. His curly white beard was like a foaming wave. The thick blue veins of his legs were like the cables of ships. His body was like a mast, and as he walked he swayed like a sailor or a boat. His eyes, like the sea itself, were sometimes blue, sometimes gray, sometimes green, and sometimes I even saw them turn violet. And he always carried two seashells in his right hand.

They were those thick white shells with brownish rings, partly rounded, partly triangular, with a hole at the triangle's vertex. Buzio passed a string through the holes, tying the two shells together, making a kind of castanet out of them. And it was with these castanets that he kept rhythm to his long, cadenced monologues, as solitary and mysterious as poetry.

Buzio would appear in the distance. One watched as he grew forth from the far reaches of sands and of roads. At first he seemed a tree or a distant boulder. But when he came closer one saw that it was Buzio.

In his left hand he carried a great stick that served as his staff; it supported him on his long walks and was his defense against the vicious dogs of the farms he passed. Attached to this stick was a bread bag in which he saved the dry pieces of bread that people gave him and the small coins. The bag was made of patched-together calico so discolored by the sun that it had almost turned white.

Buzio would arrive during the day, surrounded by light and wind, and two steps in front of him would be his old dog, faded, dirty, off-white, with thick fur, long and curly, and a black snout.

And through the streets Buzio would come, the sun on his face, the trembling shadows of sycamore leaves on his hands.

He would stop in front of a door and chant his long refrain, accompanying it with the rhythmic clicking of his seashell castanets.

The door would open and a maid in a white apron would hold out a piece of bread and say:

"Go away, Buzio."

And Buzio, ever so slowly, would take the bag from his stick, untie the strings, open the bag, and deposit his piece of bread.

And then he would go on.

He would stop beneath a balcony singing, straight and tall, while the dog sniffed the sidewalk.

And someone would lean quickly down from the balcony, so quickly one couldn't even see a face, and throw him a coin and say:

"Go away, Buzio."

And Buzio would slowly, slowly, so very slowly that one could see each individual movement, take the bag from the stick, untie the strings, open the bag, place the coin inside, once again close the bag, tie it up, and hang it from the stick.

And he would go on with his dog.

There were many poor people in that place and they would appear on Saturdays in brownish tragic bands, begging for alms and moving us to pity. There were the blind, the lame, the deaf, and the mad, there were the tubercular spitting blood into their rags, there were emaciated mothers with children almost green, there were old women, hunched and weepy, with incredibly swollen legs, there were young boys revealing their sores, their twisted arms, amputated hands, tears, misery. And above the band hovered an inexhaustible murmur of moans, plaints, prayers, and lamentations.

But Buzio would appear alone, one wouldn't know which day of the week, straight and tall, reminding one of the sea and of pine trees, and he had no wound and he didn't provoke pity. To pity him would have been like pitying a sycamore or a river or the wind. In him the barrier between man and nature seemed to have been abolished.

Buzio possessed nothing, just as a tree possesses nothing. He lived with the whole earth, and it was him as well.

The earth was his mother and his wife, his home and his company, his bed, his food, his destiny, his life.

His naked feet seemed to listen to the ground they walked upon.

And that's how I saw him appear that afternoon as I played alone in the garden.

Our house was right beside the beach.

The front part, facing the sea, had a sandy garden. In the back, facing the east, was a poorly kept, wild little garden, with small loose stones rolling beneath one's feet, a well, two trees, and a few bushes disheveled by the wind and burnt by the sun.

Buzio, coming from behind the house, pushed open the wooden gate, left it swinging, and crossed the garden without seeing me.

He stopped in front of the back door and, to the accompaniment of his seashell castanets, began to sing.

And he waited like that for a while. Then the door opened and in its dark angle an apron appeared. Seen from outside, the interior of the house seemed mysterious, shadowy and gleaming. And the maid held out a roll and said:

"Go away, Buzio."

Then she shut the door.

And Buzio, without haste, most deliberately, like someone etching each of his gestures into the light, pulled at the strings, opened the bag, tied the bag up again, hung it from the stick, and started to move off with his dog.

Then he walked around the house, to leave by the front, the side facing the sea.

And I resolved to follow him.

He crossed the sand garden covered with ice plants and sea lilies and walked off through the dunes. When he reached the spot where the bay began, he stopped. It was already a wild, deserted spot, far from any houses and roads.

I, who had followed him from a distance, came closer, hidden by the rolling dunes, and knelt down behind a tiny hillock among the dry, tall, and transparent grasses. I didn't want Buzio to see me; I wanted to see him without me, by himself.

It was a little before sunset and, now and then, a light gust of air would blow.

From high on the dune, the whole afternoon looked like an enormous transparent flower, spread wide to the horizon.

The light outlined, one by one, the hollows in the sand. The naked smell of the tidal breeze, the clean fragrance of the sea, free of dead bodies and putrefaction, was everywhere.

And all along the length of the beach, from north to south, till lost to sight, the low tide was exposing dark rocks covered with shellfish and green seaweed framing the water. And behind them, three rows of white waves were breaking incessantly, gathering up and unfolding, constantly crashing down and constantly rising again.

High on the dune stood Buzio with the afternoon. The sun had settled on his hands, on his face, and on his shoulders. He remained silent for a while, then slowly began to speak. I understood that he was talking to the sea, for he had turned toward it, holding out his open hands, cupped palms facing upward. It was a long speech, clearly articulated, irrational and mysterious, and it seemed, with the light, to sharply delineate all things.

I cannot repeat his words: I didn't memorize them and it all happened many years ago. And also I didn't entirely understand what he was saying. There were even some words I didn't quite hear, the strong wind tearing them from his mouth.

But I do remember that they were words as modulated as a song, almost visible, taking up space in the air with their shape, their density, and their weight. Words that called things forth, that were the names of things. Words that glistened like the scales of fish, words vast and clean-swept like a beach. And his words drew together the dispersed fragments of the joy of the earth. He was invoking them, showing them, naming them: wind, freshness of the waters, gold of the sun, silence and brilliance of the stars.

six

— 🙚 —

THE MAN

It was an afternoon in late November, autumn already left behind.

The city lifted up its walls of dark stone. The sky was high, desolate, the color of cold. Men walked along, jostling each other on the sidewalks. Cars passed rapidly by.

It must have been four in the afternoon of a day without sun or rain.

There were a lot of people on the street that day. I was walking rapidly along the sidewalk. At a certain moment, I found myself behind a very poorly dressed man carrying a blond child in his arms, one of those children whose beauty can barely be described. It is the beauty of a summer dawn, the beauty of a rose, the beauty of dew, all united with the incredible beauty of human innocence. Instinctively, my gaze fixed itself on the face of the child. But the man was walking very slowly and I, carried along by the bustle of the city, overtook him. But as I passed, I turned my head around to look again at the child.

It was then that I saw the man. Instantly, I came to a halt. He was an extraordinarily handsome man of about thirty, his face etched with misery, abandonment, aloneness. His suit, faded and tarnished green, allowed one to guess at the body eaten up by hunger. His hair was light brown, parted in the middle, a bit long. His beard, not cut for a long time, was growing to a point. Sharply sculpted by poverty, his face revealed the beautiful bone structure beneath. But more beautiful than anything else were his eyes, light eyes, luminous with solitude and gentleness. At the very moment I looked at him, the man raised his face to the sky.

How to describe his gesture?

It was a high sky, without an answer, the color of cold. The man raised his head in the gesture of one who, having passed beyond a certain point, no longer has anything to give and turns to the outside in search of an answer. His face dripped suffering. His expression was simultaneously one of resignation, astonishment, and questioning. He walked along slowly, very slowly, on the inside of the sidewalk, close to the wall. He held himself very straight, as if his entire body were rising up with his question. Head upturned, he looked at the sky. But the heavens were prairies of silence.

All this happened in just a moment and, as a result, I, who remember in great detail the man's suit, his face, his look, and his gestures, cannot recapture with any clarity what happened inside myself. It was as if I had turned empty as I watched the man.

The crowd continued to pass. It was the heart of the heart of the city. The man was alone, utterly alone. Rivers of people were passing by without noticing him.

Only I had stopped, but quite in vain. The man did not look at me. I wanted to do something, but I didn't know what. It was as if his solitude were beyond all of my gestures, as if it had enveloped him and separated him from me, and it was too late for any word and there was no longer any cure for anything. It was as if my hands were tied. Just as sometimes in dreams we want to act but cannot.

The man was walking very slowly. I had stopped in the middle of the sidewalk, facing the passing crowd. I could feel the city pushing me and separating me from the man. No one had seen him walking along so slowly, so very slowly, head erect and a child in his arms, close to the wall of cold stone.

Now I realize what I could have done. I would have had to decide right away. But I felt my soul and my hands weighed down with indecision. I couldn't see clearly. I was only able to hesitate and doubt. That's why I stood there, impotent, in the middle of the sidewalk. The city was pushing me and a clock struck the hour.

I remembered that someone was waiting for me and that I was late. The people who hadn't noticed the man began to notice me. It was impossible to continue standing there. Then, like a swimmer caught in a current who ceases to struggle and allows himself to go with the water's flow, I stopped opposing myself to the motion of the city and allowed myself to be carried away by the wave of people, far from the man.

But as I continued along the sidewalk surrounded by shoulders and heads, the image of the man remained suspended in my eyes. And a confused sensation grew in me that there had been something or someone in him that I had known.

Quickly I called forth all the places where I had lived. I played back the film of time in reverse. Wavering images rushed by, a bit tremulous and jerky. But I didn't find anything. I tried to reunite and reexamine all my memories of pictures, books, photographs. But the image of the man remained alone: the uplifted head gazing at the sky with an expression of infinite solitude, abandonment, questioning.

And from deep in my memory, brought forth by the image, very slowly, one by one, unmistakable, the words appeared:

"My God, my God, why hast thou forsaken me?"

Then I understood why the man I had left behind was not a

stranger. His image was exactly the same as the other image that took shape in my mind when I read:

"My God, my God, why hast thou forsaken me?"

That was it, exactly, that carriage of the head, that gaze, that suffering, that look of abandonment, that aloneness.

Beyond the hardness and betrayals of mankind, beyond the agony of the flesh, the trial of the last torment begins: the silence of God.

And the heavens seem empty and deserted above the dark cities.

I went back. I struggled against the flow of the river of people. I was afraid I had lost him. There were so many people, shoulders, heads, more shoulders. But suddenly, I saw him.

He had stopped, but he was still holding the child and gazing at the sky.

I began to run, almost shoving people aside. I was just a couple of steps away. But at that very moment, the man fell down. From his mouth flowed a river of blood and in his eyes the same expression of infinite patience remained.

The child had fallen with him and was crying in the middle of the sidewalk, hiding its face in the skirt of its blood-stained dress.

Then the crowd stopped and formed a circle around the man. Shoulders stronger than mine forced me back. I was on the outer ring of the circle. I tried to get back inside, but I couldn't. The people pressing against one another were like a single closed body. In front of me were men taller than I who prevented me from seeing. I wanted to catch a glimpse, I said "excuse me." I tried to push, but no one let me pass. I heard wailing, orders, whistles. Later I saw an ambulance. When the circle opened, the man and the child had disappeared.

Then the crowd dispersed and I remained in the middle of the sidewalk, walking on, carried along by the movement of the city.

Many years have passed. The man, no doubt, is dead. But he continues at our side. Passing through the streets.

seven

— ॐ —

THE THREE
KINGS

I. GASPAR

At that time, in the city of Kalash, Prince Zukarta established the
cult of the golden calf.

The statue settled upon the multitudes its astonished, wide-open
eyes, painted black and white. Deep in its pupils something like a
question was emerging, as if it were surprised by the extent of its
power. It was a young bull calf with small twisted horns, muscular
legs, and a short, blunt, and furrowed brow. Its four hooves, firmly
planted on the earth, gave the distinct impression of solidness and
stability, reassuring the hearts of the faithful. And all over his body
glittered gold, a compact gold: hard, heavy, dazzling.

In front of the idol, women bent down, shaking out their dark,
almost blue hair over the bright marble of the steps. From the far
reaches of the desert, from distant oases, from lost villages, men
arrived to deposit their offerings before the altar: they had come
to offer gold unto gold. And the good men of Kalash, judges and
warrior chiefs, filed reverently by in front of the bull calf. Behind
them came the merchants, the vendors, the potters, the weavers.
They kissed the steps of the altar and placed their offerings upon the
ground: they brought gold unto gold. Even the priests of the Moon

with their faithful acolytes prostrated themselves, on their knees, with their heads touching the ground, before the new idol of Kalash.

Zukarta watched all of this with great happiness, for the cult of gold was the basis of his power.

There were few who did not come running to the temple, fewer and fewer. The very poor, the shamefully destitute, the abased, didn't dare present themselves. They were like a race apart, for poverty was looked upon as the stigma of those whom the Calf did not love. Deep in their souls, so humble they scarcely dared to think their own thoughts, the very poor, the shamefully destitute, were awaiting another god.

They and Gaspar.

A delegation of important men came to Gaspar's palace. And they said:

"Why don't you present yourself at the temple of the Calf? Could it be you don't have gold to offer it? What have you in common with the rabble of the docks? Aren't you, by chance, dressed in purple and fine linen like a king? Why do you defy the power of Zukarta? Could you be a traitor? The prosperity and greatness of Kalash lies in the cult of the Calf. Have you sold yourself to our enemies?"

Gaspar answered:

"I cannot worship the power of idols. My god is different and I believe in his coming, as the Earth and the Heavens have announced to me."

Hearing this response, the tribal chieftains and the good men of Kalash said:

"We will separate ourselves from you because you have separated yourself from us and you have turned from our path. You may no longer take part in our assemblies. You will no longer be heard in our councils, nor will you partake in our festivals and banquets.

And you will also have no place in our army. Our soldiers will not protect your house or your caravans. And you will be easy prey for bandits. You will not receive the protection of our laws, and our judges will pass sentence against you, and your righteousness will be like a fistful of dust. Like the rabble, you will have neither protection nor defense until you bow at the altar of the Calf to worship the idols we worship."

And Gaspar answered:

"My god is within me like a fountain that does not flow away and he is all around me like the walls of a fortress."

Then the notables of Kalash shook the dust from their sandals and left the palace. From that day forth, many calamities fell upon Gaspar. Bandits attacked his caravans and thieves sacked his palm groves. Mysterious hands threw stones at his house during the night and in the waters of his cisterns rotten fruit and dead birds began to appear, floating on the surface.

And the time of aloneness began.

Visitors no longer came to the cool inner courtyards of the palace and the flow of water in the tanks no longer accompanied the light murmur of conversation. Relatives and friends disappeared as if swallowed by the half-light and all things seemed enveloped in scandal and terror.

However, time was growing.

And Gaspar listened to the growth of time. Solitude had created a transparent space of clarity around him in which the seconds advanced one by one and the whole universe seemed on alert. The silence was like the same word repeated endlessly.

And bent over time, Gaspar thought:

"What could grow within time if not justice?"

— 𝔞𝔳 —

Kneeling on the terrace, Gaspar gazed at the night sky. He gazed at the high, vast nocturnal vault, dark and luminous, simultaneously revealing and concealing.

And he said:

"Lord, how far away you are, how hidden and how present! I hear only the resonance of your silence that advances toward me and my life barely touches the transparent fringes of your absence. I gaze around me at the solemnity of things like someone trying to decipher a difficult script. But it is you who read me and who know me. Let nothing of my being be hidden from you. Call to your clarity the whole of my being so that my thoughts may turn transparent and I may be able to hear the word that you have always been saying to me."

At first it seemed to Gaspar that the star was a word, a word suddenly spoken in the mute attentiveness of the heavens.

But later his gaze grew accustomed to the new brilliance and he saw that it was a star, a new star, similar to other stars, but a bit closer and brighter and that it was gliding, very slowly, toward the West.

And it was to follow that star that Gaspar abandoned his palace.

II. MELCHIOR

The clay tablet had passed from generation to generation, from age to age, from hand to hand. On it was written that a redeemer would be sent to earth and that a star would rise in the East to guide those who sought his realm.

The tablet was a small rectangle of argil, blackened by time, with a fragile, wretched, worn-out look. It was a wonder that it had passed through so many centuries of opulence and collapse, of sackings, fires, and wars, without being lost. It was a wonder that it had managed to pass through the ambition, violence, turmoil, and indifference of man without being lost. There it was, in the palace, lined up beside thousands of other tablets enumerating victories, battles, massacres, and riches.

Its letters were almost effaced by time and its script was so ancient that it had become difficult to decipher with any precision. Many readings were possible.

Therefore, King Melchior called together three assemblies of wise men so that together they could ascertain the correct interpretation of that most ancient text.

First came the historians, those who had learned all the wisdom of the libraries and who were familiar to the smallest detail with the script, the language, the habits, the customs, the annals, and the codes of law of ancient times.

The assembly met for a month in the king's palace. It was the middle of summer and the heat lay heavy upon the balconies blinded by the sun. In the gardens, the palm trees creaked against each other with a metallic sound, their leaves sharp-honed and hard as the blades of saws.

Toward evening, the wise men would seat themselves in a circle in the inner courtyard of the palace. Melchior would preside. A fine trickle of water flowing through the tanks accompanied the discussions. Barefoot slaves moved about in silence, serving date-wine tempered with snow from the mountains.

The circle of seated men encompassed an empty space, and a stone table had been positioned in the center of that open area. Upon it was placed the clay tablet. It seemed extremely small and insignificant in the midst of so much space and opulence, it seemed a piece of debris from a bygone era, something left behind by time.

During thirty days of long debates, the wise men had studied and examined meticulously every line of the ancient characters.

And on the thirtieth day, Negurat, chief archivist of the temple of the Moon, arose and said:

"I believe the reading that you, oh King, have made of this text is not the true one. For you read: 'To the world a redeemer will be sent and a star will rise in the East to guide those who seek his kingdom.' But in truth the meaning of this ancient text is quite different: in fact, the characters you have read as 'redeemer,' in the remote era when this tablet was engraved, did not mean 'redeemer' but actually 'great king'; and the characters you have read as 'will be' and 'will rise' do not express future verbal forms, but rather verbal forms in the past; and the verb 'to seek' is not in the present but actually in the past perfect; and where you have read 'to guide,' it ought to read, in accord with modern methods for deciphering ancient texts 'guiding.' As a result, oh King, quite the contrary to what you thought you were reading, this text does not refer to the future but rather to the past, and it does not announce the advent of any savior, but rather glorifies the works of a great figure of long ago. And so, the correct reading of this text, in my opinion, is the following: 'To the world was sent a great king who, like a star, ruled over the East, guiding those who sought his realm.'"

When Negurat finished speaking, Atmad, the chief archivist of the palace, arose and said:

"Great is the wisdom of Negurat. But the interpretation of ancient script presents terrible difficulties. There is no doubt that in the text before us we must read 'great king' instead of 'redeemer.' However, I do not agree with what has been said about verbal forms: I believe that the verb 'to be' and the verb 'to rise' really occur in the future tense. And I also disagree with the way in which the words 'to guide,' 'to seek,' and 'kingdom' have been read. And, even further, I think that the verb 'to rise' has in this case the meaning of 'rule over.' So that, in my opinion, the correct reading of the text is this: 'Into the world a great king will be sent who like a star will rule over the East in order to exalt those people who accept his power.' For this inscription is in fact a prophecy, but a prophecy which has already been fulfilled. It is clear that the great king is the great Alexander who dominated all the East unto the kingdom of Porus and who died, as you know, in Babylon."

And when Atmad finished speaking, the learned old man Akki rose up and said:

"I am filled with admiration for the wise words that I have heard. But the truth is that the reading of this most ancient text raises so many doubts and there are so many interpretations that we could propose that, truly, oh King, we can come to no conclusion."

Then Melchior arose and said:

"Go in peace and continue your studies. I will continue to question, to listen, and to hope."

And the following month an assembly of scholars gathered in the royal palace. Melchior presented them with the doubts and the interpretations of the historians, and for thirty days the scholars studied the text.

And on the thirtieth day, toward evening, with all of them seated in a circle around the stone table upon which the clay tablet had been placed, Ken-Hur arose and said:

"Poetry doesn't express itself directly. Now the text in front of us is a poem and for this reason has to be taken as a metaphor that doesn't refer to the past or the present or the future of the world in which we live, but only to the interior world of the poet, which is the world of poetry always turned toward becoming and toward hope. This text doesn't speak of actual facts, but merely symbolizes the creative spirit of man."

Then followed Amer, who said:

"This text is a poem and lies, therefore, at the border of what is lived. The poem does not refer to that which is, but rather to that which is not. For nature is a box full of things from which the poet draws forth a thing that isn't there."

Then Amer's brother stood up and said:

"In a poem we shouldn't look for meaning, for the poem is itself its own meaning. Just as the meaning of a rose is merely that rose itself. A poem is a perfect harmony of words, a balance of syllables, a dense weight, the splendor of language, a tightly woven fabric without flaw, that only speaks of itself and, like a circle, defines its own space, and in which nothing else can possibly live. A poem doesn't mean, a poem creates."

And the discussion having ended, Melchior arose and said:

"I thank you all for your words. As for me, I will continue to seek, to listen, and to hope."

Then the scholars withdrew and the king remained alone in the courtyard, before the clay tablet, listening to the flow of water and the fall of night.

And the following month there was a gathering of wise men at the palace. Melchior presented to them the doubts of the historians and the scholars and the new assembly deliberated for thirty days.

And on the thirtieth day Kish arose and said:

"The ignorant multitudes bow down before idols, but those who think deeply know the solitude of the universe. What redeemer can we hope for? The universe is like a well-regulated machine that, without beginning or end, slowly turns through ages, eons, and cycles. In the constellations and the moons, in triangles and in circles, you will discover the laws of numbers that have proven true and that will inexorably continue to prove true. What redemption can we hope for?"

Then Maro spoke, saying:

"The gods who once existed were extinguished long ago, and what we are worshipping is merely the ashes of the divine. Who is the man, in the age in which we live, who has seen an angel? Where is one who has heard, with his own ears of flesh, the word of Isis or of Assur? We live in bereft times and everything has turned deaf and blind. In a world of injustice and disorder, we try to survive like hunted animals. The ties binding us to a watchful universe have broken. We can beat our fists upon the ground, we can implore, with our head in the dust. No one will answer us. The eye that beheld us has gone blind, the ear that heard us has shriveled. Everything is alien to us, like a place that doesn't recognize us. And the brightness of impassive stars gleams over our sadness. Who can hope that a star will move?"

Then Tot spoke, saying:

"We are born to die. All of our hopes will turn to ashes. Where is there a man who has not died? Even Alexander himself, the son of Amon, who established his empire from Egypt to the kingdom of Porus, died miserably in the palaces of Babylon. And yet his radiant youthfulness seemed to reveal the nature of a God, and his perfection was so great that no one could judge him a mortal. Who could have believed that his body, balanced and smooth as a column, his intelligence, sharp and clean as the sun, his direct gaze that made all things simple, his face brilliant as a banner, and his invincible joy would all die? Alexander, prince of Macedonia, son of Amon, the wonder of the people, carried man's destiny to its furthest limits, to such a degree that everyone assumed that in him human nature had conquered the divine. But Alexander died in the thirty-third year of his life, at the peak of his strength and his glory, in the full splendor of his youth. And thus the gods have told us that man cannot overcome his destiny and that his destiny is the destiny of death. Therefore, oh King, what can we hope for? Nothing can change the human condition and in that condition there is no place for hope."

When the wise men had retired, Melchior rose from his throne and approached the stone table. In the midst of the tall columns that surrounded the courtyard, the clay tablet seemed extremely fragile and small. But the king pressed his brow to the almost obliterated letters.

That night, after the Moon had disappeared behind the mountains, Melchior went up to the balcony and saw that in the sky, to the East, there was a new star.

The city was asleep, dark and silent, enveloped in its narrow streets and confusion of stairways. No one was walking any longer along the broad avenue of the temples. All that could be heard, from time to time, coming from the walls, were the cries of the sentinels making their rounds.

And above the world of sleep, above the tangled shadow of dreams in which men were lost groping, as if in a thick, humid, shifting labyrinth, the star, young, tremulous, and bedazzled, was igniting its joy.

And Melchior left his palace that very night.

III. BALTHAZAR

King Balthazar loved the freshness of his gardens and smiled to see the reflection of his ebony face in the clear water of the tanks.

And he loved the joyfulness, the commotion, and the abundance of banquets, and often his parties lasted till daybreak.

However, late one night, after all the guests had withdrawn, the king remained in the great hall, alone with a young slave who was playing the flute.

And it seemed to him that the melody was sketching in the air the outline of an empty space.

Then his heart grew heavy with sorrow, and Balthazar thought: "Could it be that one day I will retire from life like a satiated guest withdrawing from a banquet? Or will I always have the same thirst, the same hunger, the same desire for each moment and each day?"

And having thought this, he passed through the door of the hall and went out into the garden.

Out there, in the uncertain light of predawn, the garden seemed to float suspended. The mist obscured the clear outline of the tanks and diluted the shapes of foliage in the air. Balthazar walked at length between the flowers and the palm trees until the sun came up. And when it was already daylight, he came to a small balcony at the far end of the garden. He leaned over the parapet and, there on the other side of the narrow street, he saw a young man, leaning against a wall, looking at him.

Balthazar stood motionless as if the other man's face had hit him in the face. Or as if the face of the other had suddenly become his own. Or as if, for the first time in his life, he had seen the face of another man.

What had surprised him most in that face was its nakedness, its naked clarity. It was as if in that face the ceremony of life had removed its mask and reality had revealed, without any veil, the forlornness, the conscious pain, the essential condition of man.

It was the face of a thin young man, in which the bones revealed, with no equivocation, the ideogram of hunger. Sorrow rose from memory's deepest dwelling place and emerged, complete, on the surface of the pupils. Patience, like a dusting of ash, had settled upon his brow, his lips, his shoulders. And in this patience there was such tenderness that Balthazar felt a sudden sharp desire to cry and prostrate himself with his face pressed to the ground.

And he asked:

"You, who are you?"

"I am hungry," the man murmured.

"Come in," said Balthazar. "I will command that they serve you the best fruits, the best meats, the best wines. I will order them to wash your feet with perfumed water in a golden basin. I will command that they dress you in purple. I will order my musicians to play for your pleasure the most beautiful melodies. I will order the cittern player to come to you. I myself will place beneath your feet the most precious of tapestries, and I will sit at your side to free you from your solitude, and I will listen to your words so that you may partake of joy and so that the fountains and gardens of this palace may extinguish your sorrow."

However, the man, hearing these words, became frightened. In the black face, leaning down in the white light of the balcony, he recognized with terror the face of the king. And he thought:

"Oh, no! Why has the king called to me? I was looking at his palace and that, for sure, is a crime. I better flee before the guards get here."

For that man, like all the very poor, knew that the world was governed by laws that persecuted them and condemned them, and for this reason he was afraid at any moment of being accused and arrested for some unknown reason. He was passing through a country that wasn't his own and where everything for him spelled insecurity and fear.

And therefore he fled and disappeared panting among the curves of the narrow little street, without seeing the gesture with which Balthazar was beckoning to him.

And in the palace the king said to his guards:

"Go forth and seek through the streets for a thin young man, dressed in rags, and his eyes filled with patience and sorrow."

However, toward evening the guards returned and said:

"We found so many men in rags, sad and patient, that we didn't know how to pick out the one you are looking for."

And so, the next morning, King Balthazar, having taken off his purple robes, wrapped himself in a cloak of common cloth and left the palace, alone, in search of the man.

He descended through narrow sloping streets and, far from the triumphal great avenues where the breeze made the hard leaves of the palm trees rustle, he searched at length through the poor neighborhoods alongside the river. The stevedores of the docks lifted their dark faces toward him, and a man selling cord sandals rested his tired gaze on that of the king. He saw men doubled under their burdens, he saw those who pulled carts like oxen, slow and patient as oxen, he saw those who wore shackles on their feet, he saw those who glided close to the walls, as silent as shadows, he saw those who screamed, those who cried, those who moaned. He saw those who stood alone, motionless, leaning against the walls, dazed, questioning, beyond the hoarse cry of the streets, the opaque silence, staring ahead at the straight road of silence. He saw those who caught small fish in the dirty waters of the river. He saw those with faces the color of rags and hands the color of ash, ash so light it would fly with the wind. He saw the green shadows, the kingdom of patience, the country of endless desolation, the realm of the abased, the left side of life, the land of the dispossessed, the bottom of the sea of the city.

And on the following day, the king called together his ministers and said to them:

"Give orders for the distribution of my treasures and the distribution of the reserves gathered in our storehouses and our granaries. And divide all of it among the hungry and the poor who beg."

Having heard this, the ministers withdrew to deliberate.

And after three days they returned and they answered:

"Your treasures are insufficient to ransom all the slaves, and the reserves in your storehouses do not suffice to appease the hungry. Not even your power is enough to alter the order of the city. If we do as you have commanded, the foundations that support us and the walls that protect us will crumble. Your desire goes against the good of the kingdom."

And the king answered:

"I seek another law, I seek another kingdom."

Then the ministers withdrew, whispering among themselves:

"It will come to pass that he will betray us."

On the following day, Balthazar made his way to the temple of all the gods.

And he read these words engraved on the stone of the first altar:

"I am the god of the strong, and to those who invoke me I give power and dominion; they will never be defeated and they will be feared like gods."

The king went on to the second altar and he read:

"I am the goddess of fertile land, and to those who worship me I give vigor, abundance, and fecundity, and they will be as beautiful and happy as the gods."

The king passed on to the third altar and he read:

"I am the god of wisdom and to those who worship me I give an agile and subtle spirit, a clear intelligence, and the science of numbers. They will rule the arts and the crafts, and they will be as proud as the gods of the works they create."

And having passed before the three altars, Balthazar asked the priests:

"Tell me where the altar is of the god who protects the meek and the oppressed, so that I can pray to him and worship him."

At the end of a long silence, the priests answered:

"Of that god we know nothing."

That night, King Balthazar, after the Moon had disappeared behind the mountains, climbed to the highest of his balconies and said:

"Lord, I see. I see the flesh of suffering, the face of humility, the look of patience. And how can one who has seen these things not see you? And how can I bear what I have seen if I don't come unto you?"

The star rose very slowly into the sky, to the East. Its motion was almost imperceptible. It seemed to be very close to the earth. It glided silently along, and not a leaf was stirring. It had been coming forever. It revealed joy, the wholeness of joy, without imperfection, the seamless vestments of joy, the immortal substance of joy.

And Balthazar recognized it immediately, for it could not have been otherwise.

ADAMASTOR SERIES

— ❦ —

Series Editor: Anna M. Klobucka

Chaos and Splendor & Other Essays
Eduardo Lourenço
Edited by Carlos Veloso

Producing Presences:
Branching Out from Gumbrecht's Work
Edited by Victor K. Mendes and
João Cezar de Castro Rocha

Sonnets and Other Poems
Luís de Camões
Translated by Richard Zenith

The Traveling Eye: Retrospection, Vision,
and Prophecy in the Portuguese Renaissance
Fernando Gil and Helder Macedo
Translated by K. David Jackson, Anna M. Klobucka,
Kenneth Krabbenhoft, Richard Zenith

The Sermon of Saint Anthony to the Fish and Other Texts
António Vieira
Translated by Gregory Rabassa

The Correspondence
of Fradique Mendes: A Novel
José de Maria de Eça de Queirós
Translated by Gregory Rabassa

The Relic: A Novel
José de Maria de Eça de Queirós
Preface by Harold Bloom
Translated by Aubrey F. G. Bell

Maiden and Modest:
A Renaissance Pastoral Romance
Bernardim Ribeiro
Foreword by Earl E. Fitz
Translated by Gregory Rabassa

Saint Christopher: A Novella
José de Maria de Eça de Queirós
Foreword by Carlos Reis
Translated by Gregory Rabassa
and Earl E. Fitz

Exemplary Tales
Sophia de Mello Breyner Andresen
Introduction by Cláudia Pazos-Alonso
Translated by Alexis Levitin